BEYOND
THE
DARKNESS

A CALL TO JOY

MAREE STUARTT

www.mareestuartt.com

ISBN:
Paperback
978-1-64184-445-1
Ebook
978-1-64184-446-8

Published by: Maree Stuartt

First edition 2021

Printed in the USA.

*"Find a place where there is joy,
and the joy will burnout the pain."*

Joseph Campbell

∞ DEDICATION ∞

I dedicate this book to those of you, who may have felt disconnected, lonely and even trapped in a life that you don't love.
Perhaps you have longed for a sense of belonging, of being understood or just wanted to be happy. May you employ your strength
and courage to "Call to Joy" and create a life you love through
your thoughts, words and actions.

May we all embrace life in our darkest hours and live with Joy.

∞ PREFACE ∞

This story is fiction; however, they are a few things in the book that are true. The main one is the angel; When you learn how she mysteriously shows up, I'm sure it will intrigue you, as it still does me to this day.

I trust the presence of the angel and the vibration of the words touch you deeply, enlightening in you the belief that life is worth living through your darkest hours. Even if it is an escape from your current life, may your heart and mind be wrapped in a world of love, hope and magic, knowing that everything is working out in your highest good. Always knowing this or something better is coming your way.

Thank you for taking the time to pick up this book, may you be blessed with healing in whatever area in your life you need it the most. Words are powerful, and the art of storytelling is a gift thank you for reading this story.

∞ ACKNOWLEDGEMENTS ∞

I am in awe of this wooden angel who mysteriously showed up in my life years ago, nudging me to write. This angel gives me hope and trust in the magic of life as it unfolds.

Greg, my loving husband, you are my inspiration, showing me, anything is possible. Thank you for continuously supporting my quirkiness and allowing me to follow my curiosity. You are my earth angel.

Massive thanks to all my friends and family who continuously encourage me along this journey. Without your love and support, this book would not have come to fruition.

Tom Bird, thank you for sharing your wisdom and holding a safe space guiding me to trust and cultivate writing from my heart. I appreciate your craft and thank your staff for all their encouragement.

Creating a book from a written manuscript takes a team. I am grateful for all those involved in editing, formatting, designing, publishing and circulating this book so that the wisdom will reach those who need it.

Thank you, the reader who followed your inspiration in choosing this book. Allow yourself to receive the wonderful insights, and may your heart be expanded with Joy.

∞ CONTENTS ∞

∞ 1 ∞

THE SPIRAL BEGINS

TAHLIA WANDERED AIMLESSLY, trapped in a bustling marketplace, hemmed in by a maze of stalls, plants, and animals. Store owners were peddling their stock loudly in her ear, thrusting colorful fabrics toward her as she passed by. Wafting smells of spices, exotic food, sweet perfume, and animal feces violated her sensitive nose. An overwhelming oppressive heat was taunting her. Disorientated and feeling unwell, Tahlia was desperately trying to get out, to find some air, some relief from all the loud noise and chaos.

Suddenly Tahlia locked her gaze onto the most alluring blue eyes she had ever seen. It's as if they were piercing straight through her, mesmerizing her, entrapping her in a feeling of exquisite beauty, something so beautiful it took her breath away. This feeling was like nothing she had ever felt before, such a stark contrast to the hectic chaos around her.

Tahlia stood there motionless; time suspended as she bathed in this feeling. These penetrating blue eyes transfixed her, both their beauty and sense of freedom filling her with intrigue and curiosity. In a flash, the eyes were on the move, weaving so quickly through the market stalls. Tahlia found herself magnetized to follow. Who do these eyes belong to? Tahlia's curiosity nudged at her. Frantically pushing and pulling her way past the chattering crowds, she ignored the steamy heat as her temperature was rising.

Tahlia desperately tried to catch up to the elusive beauty that the eyes were emanating, feeling an inner craving for the freedom they were offering. Tahlia kept searching, looking everywhere, clumsily knocking into stall owners, scanning their faces, none of them belonging to those eyes. Tahlia moved on as the stall owners hurled abuse at her.

From out of nowhere, a hand grabbed Tahlia; her entire body trembled, vibrating uncontrollably, an incredible energy coursing through her. Instantaneously Tahlia was transported to the top of a mountain cliff, extremely high, so high she felt as if she could almost touch the sky. Tahlia gasped; in front of her lay the most magnificent vista: mountains and valleys encapsulated with tropical vegetation and large cliff faces. The subtle smell of freshly cut grass on rolling green hills in the distance, leading her vision to massive old trees curving along the banks of a river flowing toward an aqua-blue ocean. The expansive blue sky appeared to stretch for miles before blending into the sea. The view was breathtaking. Tahlia momentarily closed her eyes to breathe it all in. As she blinked, her eyes opened; appearing directly in front of her were those alluring blue eyes, peeking out from under a veil of sheer cotton fabric. Tahlia noticed a very faint outline of a body under the thin cotton wrapping; she couldn't make it out because the beauty of those eyes entrapped her focus. Tahlia sensed them encouraging her in a soft voice:

"Tahlia, it's time to break free from feeling trapped, lonely, bored, in life. It's time to feel loved and to trust the flow of life; come be free, be happy."

Tahlia hungered for a new life, full of fun and adventure. Oh, how she wished she could trust enough, to jump, to follow those eyes!

Instead, Tahlia became paralyzed by fear; her inner voice telling her she wasn't good enough and didn't deserve to be happy. A tear rolled down Tahlia's face; part of her felt she would never have the courage to take that leap.

At that moment, Tahlia's attention became drawn to her aching feet. Peering down, Tahlia realized she was balancing on a very narrow rock perched on the apex of this mountain cliff. Without warning, the rock started to move. Tahlia lost her balance, free-falling.

She screamed, as fear engaged every part of her body, tumbling face-first down the side of the massive cliff. Visions of the past filled her mind. Thoughts of not feeling good enough, girls at school bullying her, telling her that she was useless, she would never amount to anything.

"You're weird, you look funny, stop trying to be so special, you'll never be one of us," the voices chanted.

"Idiot, you're so clumsy, always making silly mistakes, you can't do anything right," were words she had often spoken to herself. "Get out of your imagination; you'll never amount to anything; you're not good enough." All these nasty words and thoughts were pummeling Tahlia as she kept tumbling. Wanting to free herself, Tahlia screamed hysterically: "ENOUGH!"

All of a sudden, the faces of Tahlia's loved ones began flashing past her. Her nan, pop, mum, dad, brother, sister, all her friends, a montage of happy faces flashing by as she continued tumbling. As the speed of Tahlia's free-fall quickened, it dawned on her: This is it. I'm dying! Tahlia couldn't believe her life was coming to an end; she hadn't meant it to be this way.

"It can't be the end; all I wanted was freedom." Tahlia heard the words vibrating through her.

Focusing on the faces of her family and friends, she opened her heart, radiating love to them all.

"I'm so sorry; I truly love you with my whole heart. Please forgive me, I didn't mean to hurt you. Please know that I love you." Tahlia desperately reached out, grasping for their hands, a piece of clothing, anything, as she continued to fall, thinking, *All I can do is go with the flow.*

Instantly a gentle peace enveloped Tahlia, like an angel wrapping its wings around her. Tahlia completely let go, collapsing into this incredible serene feeling, noticing a tingling vibration from the crown of her head down her entire body. Surrendering,

Tahlia saw herself pulled into a brilliant welcoming white light. "Go with the flow, go with the flow," she heard herself repeating.

***

Lying frozen stiff, Tahlia opened her eyes, adjusting them to the light, peering around, sensing a familiarity. *Was she in her bed?* Utterly confused, caught between both worlds, Tahlia contemplated, *Where am I? Am I alive or dead?* Her thoughts flickered, searching for an answer; *What happened?* Foggy and dazed, Tahlia vaguely remembered trying to suffocate herself with her pillow. *I'm sure I took enough pills and vodka! What was that whole free-fall thing I just experienced? Those eyes; who did they belong to?*

Utterly perplexed by her scrambled thoughts, Tahlia summoned up the will, touching her body to see if she could feel her skin, pinching it hard. "OUCH!"

Tahlia rolled her head slowly toward her bedside table, looking for signs. She observed a knocked-over pill bottle, surrounded by a scattering of white pills, a large empty crystal water jug containing only a small remnant of straight vodka. Sniffing the jug, Tahlia smirked to herself. She had been clever putting the vodka in a crystal glass jug so that if anyone found her, they wouldn't assume it was vodka. It was evident to Tahlia that she had drunk most of the vodka. However, she couldn't be sure how many pills she had consumed, as there appeared to be a vast number still lying on the bedside table.

As Tahlia slowly turned her head to the other side of her bed, she noticed red lipstick smeared all over her pillowcase. A vague recollection of burying her face in the pillow, trying to suffocate herself, filled her vision. Tahlia winced.

It was clear to Tahlia she had intentionally tried to end her life, *so what went wrong?* Staring at the white ceiling in a haze of disbelief, Tahlia became entangled in her thoughts. Perhaps *this was how it was; you get to see the last moments of your life before a loud booming voice commands, "Please enter the pearly gates of heaven to the right. Oh, so sorry you weren't good enough this life, it's hell for you, off to the left."*

Tahlia laid there anxiously, waiting for someone to say something. Nothing!

A sickening feeling washed over Tahlia, forcing her to sit up. She clutched the bedsheets; her knuckles turned white as she fought the desire to vomit. Once the nausea passed, Tahlia gingerly attempted to place one foot on the carpet beside her bed. She sincerely hoped she couldn't feel the ground, not wanting it to be real. The soul of her foot felt the firmness of the carpet underfoot. *Damn,* she thought as her other foot followed. *What now?* Another wave of nausea flooded through her. "Stand up," Tahlia sheepishly ordered her body. She found herself instantly standing, but the room was spinning. Heaving and gagging, Tahlia raced to the bathroom toilet, projectile-vomiting into the bowl. It felt as if her entire insides were coming up, splattering everywhere. The reality was settling in with every heave. Tahlia knelt there clinging to the bowl, exhausted, her berating thoughts running wild, *I can't believe this; I can't even succeed at killing myself. Am I ever going to do anything good enough in this damn life?*

Tahlia's frustration grew, making her agitated. She felt she needed to move. Mustering all her strength, Tahlia managed to stand holding onto the vanity, mumbling insanities to herself in the mirror. She shouldn't be looking in the mirror this morning; she was hoping to see the pearly gates of heaven or even the red-hot flames of hell. However, here she was in her living hell. Staring back at her, a mascara-streaked face, remnants of red smeared lipstick everywhere, messy hair, eyes that seemed dull and lifeless.

"Stupid girl, you've certainly made a good botch-up of this. You're never good enough." Tahlia's inner voice scolded her, sending an uncomfortable shiver down her spine.

Consumed in a self-criticizing rant about her failed suicide attempt, Tahlia suddenly felt something brush past her face. Jolting her out of her self-obsessed thoughts, gazing into the mirror, she saw those piercing blue eyes – the same eyes she had seen in the marketplace. Confusion swept over her; Tahlia couldn't comprehend what was happening. *Those alluring eyes weren't they part of my altered state: the markets, the free-fall, the suicide?* Everything seemed hazy and blurred. Tahlia stared at those eyes in the mirror, witnessing their exquisite beauty peering back at her. They beckoned Tahlia to a happy place of love, freedom, excitement – something she had craved for so long. Tahlia felt tears pouring down her face, the immense beauty triggering all her pain inside. Tahlia's heart was aching, cracking open with every sob reverberating throughout her body.

Eventually, the sobs softened. Tahlia came to accept she indeed was alive; much to her dismay, she would have to face another day on earth, living.

In a trance-like state, turning on the shower, Tahlia said aloud, "No one ever needs to know about this. You are alive, just pretend nothing happened."

Tahlia immersed herself in the running water, feeling it stream over her body. She made the shower extra hot today as she wanted the steaming water to wash it all away. "It" being all those painful thoughts, including any remnants of her failed suicide.

Tahlia eventually stepped out of the shower. Lacking all enthusiasm, she tried encouraging herself. "Come on, girl, get it together, you know the usual boring old routine; get ready, put on a fake smile, head to work, blah, blah, blah."

As Tahlia dried herself, she felt trapped in the merry go round of life. *Surely there is something more than this tedious grind; I'm so fed up.* Staring at her own bloodshot eyes in the mirror, she asked herself, in a commanding voice, "What can I do differently to feel peace with this thing called life? What can I do to manifest a life I truly love and enjoy?"

Sighing deeply, Tahlia moved away from the mirror, nursing her aching head, observing the mess in her room. In a slow daze, Tahlia dressed for work, pulling on faded jeans and a neutral-colored top. Tahlia made minimal effort to apply her makeup, a quick swipe of bronzer across her eyes and cheeks, adding some mascara. After all, she had to disguise her blurry red eyes somehow.

A fleeting vision flashed into Tahlia's mind. She saw herself drinking all the vodka, reaching out for the pill bottle, but couldn't recall taking any pills.

Beginning to feel ghastly hungover and dehydrated, Tahlia meandered into the kitchen, searching for some headache tablets. Tahlia knew calling in sick wouldn't be an option; she didn't want to arouse any suspicion, especially from Helena, her best friend.

Popping a few tablets in her mouth, Tahlia guzzled a large glass of water. *Ahh, relief,* she thought as she placed the rest of the packet in her handbag, knowing she definitely would need them throughout the day. Not sure if she was hungry, Tahlia grabbed a bagel from the fridge, wrapping it in a napkin. Looking at her clock, somewhat surprised, she realized she had time to walk to work. So, Tahlia headed off on foot rather than her usual Uber rush. Instinctively, she knew walking would burn off some of her frustrations. Tahlia felt the need to do things differently today; after all, she wasn't even supposed to be here, that wasn't the plan. Somehow it seemed life had a different idea for her.

∞ 2 ∞
WHAT NOW

TAHLIA WAS 27, a smart, fit, healthy blonde who always loved to look and feel good, emanating an innocent, sweet beauty. Her adventurous spirit developed when she was young, as she often explored her vivid imagination, delighting in fantasies and stories. Tahlia used to believe in the magic of life, feeling a magical undercurrent and approaching every day with awe and wonderment.

Her fascination with the magic of life led Tahlia to explore quantum physics and the healing arts, dabbling in a few herself. She knew for sure there had to be a better way to do this thing called life. Through her quest to explore and experience life to the fullest, she began traveling extensively, exploring different cultures. Traveling made her happy and connected her to something grander than life itself.

Being fueled by her travel adventures, imagination, and loving the art of storytelling, Tahlia naturally fell into a career she loved, as a script writer for Disney. Adoring movies and being immersed in these creative worlds, Tahlia loved the scale of emotions and senses a good film provoked. This feeling inspired Tahlia to apply herself 100% with an inner confidence shining through everything she did.

Tahlia was super sensitive and found that when the harsh reality and contrasts of living would take over, she couldn't help but wonder why there was so much pain and suffering, sometimes seeing life as cruel and unfair. As a child, she often felt the pain of those who hurt themselves. This sensitivity was painful and heart-breaking to Tahlia, so she learned to block it out, ignoring her gut feelings and putting her faith in others, listening to them rather than to her own heart. Even though she trusted in something grander than herself, the fact that Tahlia blocked out her sensitivity manifested in a tendency to control things, sometimes forcing things to work out the way she wanted.

Struggling with life, Tahlia had often thought about suicide, especially in her younger years. Tahlia felt she was a total misfit and thought it would be better for everyone if she departed this planet. Being a teenager had been hard; she had found others downright cruel at times, especially the girls. Weren't they all supposed to bond together; you know girl power, better together, wasn't that the slogan at school? However, this didn't appear to be the case, as she witnessed girls putting each other down and robbing each other of their confidence. Tahlia cringed at their hurtful remarks.

"Look at you, la-de-dah. Who do you think you are, all dressed up? Didn't you look in the mirror before you came out? You're so weird."

Growing into her 20's, Tahlia found it to be even worse. Everyone competing with each other, social media becoming a minefield for self-judgment and comparisons, never feeling enough. Perhaps all this was part of what led Tahlia to the decision the previous night to end her life. Tahlia was fed up with existing in a world that was so cruel and unfair. Her vitality had diminished, and she didn't even know where she fit in anymore. Tahlia was lonely, bored and exhausted, she had had enough of suffering. Tahlia desperately wanted to escape all of it, hence the rather lame attempt at ending her life. She remembered saying to herself in the last minute:

"Okay, here goes; if I succeed, fantastic, I'll be free; if I wake up in the morning, then perhaps I'm meant to be here." Unbelievably, Tahlia had woken up. *What now? How am I ever going to get through today, through life*, she thought, rubbing her aching head?

At the office, Tahlia sheepishly walked toward her desk, diverting her gaze towards the floor in case someone noticed her puffy eyes.

"Morning, my beautiful friend!" said Helena.

Helena was Tahlia's best friend, a loving, warm person who was always there for Tahlia. Helena was one of those friends everyone craves, a faithful buddy who loves you no matter what, yet was willing to tell you the truth. Helena accepted Tahlia for who she was, never allowing her to go off track for too long without gently pulling her back. They shared a fun and happy relationship; both believed in magic, together finding magic in everything they did. Usually, these two together were loads of fun to be around, although of late Helena noticed that Tahlia had lost her zest for life and was somewhat insular.

Seeing Tahlia hiding her face, Helena stopped in her tracks, sensing something was up. "What has happened to you, Tahlia?"

"Nothing, it was a rough night, just didn't sleep well. Too much on my mind, you know what it's like."

"Okay," Helena replied, a little suspicious. Surely Tahlia felt safe enough to tell her everything; they had been friends for years. "Maybe we can do lunch," Helena called over her shoulder as Tahlia walked away.

"Sure," Tahlia nodded, settling herself at her desk, burying her head into work, praying no one else would come to disturb her. Today was going to be a very long day.

Tahlia opened her computer, and like most other mornings, found herself swamped with emails. Tahlia tried to focus, doing her best not to reflect on last night, the reality of everything syncing in. As Tahlia stared at the screen, her vision blurred, everything faded to black.

Tahlia's head landed softly on her desk, instantly transporting her to another time and place that somehow felt familiar, yet everything appeared different.

Seeing herself, a fragile young woman, shivering, lying on the cobblestone walkway in front of a small stone house, supporting a steep sloping roof and blue painted wooden shutters. She was battered and bruised, lonely, struggling to breathe, not knowing what to do. Her life was in ruins, running away had taken its toll on her, she had no more energy to go on, no will to live. Willing to give up, she had crossed the edge of caring, life was way too hard. If this was all life is, what is the point? She lay there, hoping to die.

At that moment, an older man bent down and gently wrapped Tahlia in a warm coat. He picked her up and carried her inside his French cottage, reassuring her that all was well. Tahlia recognized a delicate beauty in his eyes, feeling safe, she allowed herself to sink into his arms.

Ivan placed the fragile young women on his lounge, wrapping her in his favorite blanket, ensuring her comfort. Holding her hand, he watched as she peacefully fell asleep.

Ivan's house was humble, yet full of eclectic artifacts, collected throughout his lifetime from many different adventures.

Looking at the young woman on his sofa, Ivan noted an uncanny resemblance to his late daughter, Madeleine. Ivan saw his daughter's face; she was young and seemed carefree; he loved her breeziness, her lightness that had added joy to his days, until that fatal day.

Madeleine had committed suicide. He found her hanging from a tree – a sight he would never ever forget. The pain had dug so deep into Ivan's heart, ripping his entire lifeforce out of his body. He had already lost his loving wife, Amelie, and now Madeleine. Ivan's life spun out of control for a while after that, yet somehow the wounds had healed, leaving only scars, two reminders of the love he once knew. Looking down at this girl on his sofa, he felt a twinge of pain enter him like someone was sticking a sharp knife into that scar. Tears trickled down his face; her name rolled off his tongue: "Madeleine."

Tahlia awoke disorientated on Ivan's sofa; not knowing whether to be grateful or angry, she was ready to die, yet the warmth of the blanket on her skin felt comforting.

Noticing the older man standing over her crying, Tahlia instinctively pulled her hand from under the warm blanket and raised her fingers to touch his arm in comfort. Their eyes met, emanating an undercurrent of sadness yet compassionate understanding.

Ivan cleared his throat, apologizing in his French accent, "I'm sorry; you remind me of my daughter, Madeleine. She has passed, she committed suicide."

Tahlia could see and feel his pain; she wanted to give him a big hug, yet was frozen and found words falling out her mouth, "What happened?" Tahlia cringed; it was none of her business.

Ivan sighed; he couldn't believe he was about to tell a total stranger about his deepest wound.

"My daughter, Madeleine, she was just like you, a pretty young thing, always seemed happy on the outside, yet I had no idea she felt tormented; inside her was so much pain. Her mother, Amelie, died from cancer when she was young; it was just Madeleine and me.

"She was a smart, funny girl, and we seemed to have good times together. I worked hard, as I wanted her to have the best I could provide for her. I honestly thought she was happy…." His voice trailed off as the sadness flooded his heart.

"I'm sorry," he said, his voice quivering in-between tears that were flowing. "I found Madeleine hanging, in the tree out there in the back yard. Such a waste of a beautiful life."

Tahlia couldn't believe what she was hearing. "I'm so sorry, that must have been terrible, so painful." Tahlia couldn't imagine the pain this man had felt, losing everything that was so precious to him. How could he still even have a will to live?

Long moments of silence between them felt like eons, "It was one of the worst moments of my life," said Ivan, breaking the uncomfortable silence.

Tahlia had been in that same place, where she wanted to die, to take her own life. Sensing Ivan's pain, Tahlia flashed back to a scene of her own family. Her loving mother and father were doing their best as life unfolded in front of them, working, raising the kids, feeling the stress of life, and lack of time. Tahlia assumed her parents loved each other even though they had a strange way of showing it, often reacting through frustration. Tahlia remembered running away as she couldn't handle it all; the arguments, the lack of joy. All she wanted was to feel happy.

Tahlia's attention returned to the troubled man in front of her, pouring his heart out. What if he had known that her wish that day were to also die. This kind man, a total stranger, had gracefully saved her. At that moment, Tahlia's heart opened with deep compassion. Tahlia felt the incredible pain and suffering that suicide causes those who love you, realizing how devastating it is for everyone when you give up on your soul.

"I'm so sorry for your loss; my name is Tahlia," she said, stretching out her hand.

His face warmed with a smile, "I'm Ivan. Would you like a hot chocolate and some warm soup?"

Tahlia nodded. She could feel Ivan was a kind, caring soul and wanted to make her comfortable.

"Stay covered up and gather your strength. Tahlia, you have a wonderful life ahead of you."

How odd, Tahlia thought, how did that man know she had been feeling lonely and disconnected, that she had given up on life? Deep inside, Tahlia was craving to feel an enthusiasm for life, a connection that bought her joy and freedom. Was it possible; could she really have the wonderful life she dreamed of?

***

"Tahlia, Tahlia," Helena was shaking her. "Come on; its lunchtime, let's go for a walk." Helena was used to Tahlia slumped over her desk; it must have been another one of "those visions" Tahlia was always having.

Tahlia shook her head, doing her best to focus on Helena's voice. Tahlia's visions had become so life-like recently; she had trouble deciding what was real and what was not. Maybe someone was trying to tell her something?

As Tahlia and Helena walked out into the street, Tahlia was hoping she wouldn't have to explain to Helena about her suicide attempt last night. Tahlia was feeling pretty rough and fragile; she still had a massive headache and was starting to feel guilty and ashamed that she had even attempted to end her life.

"Why didn't you sleep last night, Tahlia?" Helena asked.

Tahlia stumbled for words, "Oh, um, just everything seemed to get on top of me. Maybe the moon was affecting my emotions. You know how it can sometimes be."

"Yeah, sometimes our monkey minds can play havoc," agreed Helena.

Phew, thought Tahlia. *Hopefully, I have deflected the conversation.*

Walking into Mr. Wong's sushi, they found a quiet table and sat down for lunch.

"Helena, do you think we can have a wonderful life full of happiness?" asked Tahlia, wanting to change the subject.

"Of course I do, aren't we?" replied Helena, a little confused, as Tahlia had been her friend who always believed in the magic of life and that anything was possible.

"Helena, if we are one hundred percent honest, are we truly happy?"

Helena pondered the question for a moment, "I would say yes, especially compared to many others." Helena was a close enough friend to detect something was odd with Tahlia; there was an underlying sadness in her friend. "What's happened to you, Tahlia?"

Tahlia diverted her gaze to her food, pushing it around with her chopsticks. "Nothing."

"Did you have a big night on the town last night, Tahlia? Because you sure look like it."

"No, no, I told you I tossed and turned all night, with wild, crazy dreams. Although in all honesty, it does feel like I've been on a bender."

Helena was not convinced, but didn't want to push Tahlia, as she could feel her fragility.

"Okay, as long as you are all right, Tahlia, as we all know the power of your vivid imagination," Helena laughed.

Tahlia laughed for the first time that day, "Yes indeed, bizarre dreams, falling off cliffs, floating through space, a whole jumble of things."

Helena raised her eyebrows, "It's a shame we can't make our dreams be what we want. You know, like our wildest fantasies coming true."

Tahlia laughed again; Helena's enthusiasm could always make her laugh. They ate lunch, Tahlia slowly savoring every bite, and each belly laugh with Helena.

They returned to the office, Tahlia feeling slightly better, having escaped telling her best friend what she had tried to do the night before.

Helena knew there was more to what Tahlia was telling her but would leave it for now. Helena felt satisfied she had inspired a smile back to Tahlia's face.

∞ 3 ∞

ESCAPE THE GRIND

AS TAHLIA'S DAY continued, a roller-coaster of emotions and thoughts kept rolling through her head. *How could I have been so stupid? Didn't I take more than enough pills? Wouldn't it have been much better for all if I wasn't here? How selfish, did I truly want to inflict more pain onto my family and friends?* There didn't seem to be any space between these bombarding, conflicting thoughts.

Tahlia decided she needed to move, so she took a walk to the bathroom; perhaps the sheer act of moving would free her from her mind. On the way, passing by a window, Tahlia stopped to glance out. The office overlooked a lovely green park with a water fountain falling into a large pond. It was a hive of activity; people walking around the lake in the sun, kids playing, chasing each other, dogs barking, tree branches swaying in the breeze. Tahlia allowed herself to melt into the vista. Observing the moment led her back to her grandfather and hanging out with him on his farm. Her grandfather had been so in tune with nature and the cycles that it brought. He loved and respected all the elements: the rain which he believed cleansed and refreshed the land, the burning fires, sometimes leaving devastation yet always clearing a way for new life. A windy day, which grandpa always referred to as shaking and clearing away the debris. The warming sun, filtering energy and vitality into everything, his favorite on a cold winter's day. Tahlia had loved experiencing those moments with him; they made her feel so alive.

Caleb tapped Tahlia on the shoulder, she reacted almost jumping out of her skin, catching herself from falling over.

"Sorry to startle you, Tahlia, but here's another script that needs amending. The head honcho wants it tightened up, asap. You know, like now," he added sarcastically.

Tahlia stumbled for words; not sure she could handle that type of stress today. "Caleb, can you please ask for an extension. I'm not feeling well."

Already walking away, Caleb raised his hands as if to say, not my problem.

Caleb was a sweet millennial yet extremely driven to work his way up the company ladder. He had become their boss's puppet. She wondered if Caleb was happy, always allowing someone else to pull his strings. Tahlia hoped one day he would come into his own and not become a mirror image of someone else or fall victim to someone else's dream.

Back at her desk, Tahlia was barely coping; she felt overwhelmed with her workload and her thoughts.

Tahlia looked around at everyone pumping out scripts. Was this the new art of telling stories, the same old format over and over again? Stories made just for visual entertainment, no profound messages. Did the audience even care if a film contained a message? How many people watched countless movies without even registering that the film or story had touched them on some level.

Tahlia thought about all the energy that went into writing scripts, developing them, and turning them into movies. She believed all the power behind creating, writing, editing, producing, was transferred into people working on the film and, in turn, filtered out to the audience. What thoughts and energy were all her co-workers funneling into them? There had to be a better way of telling stories, a way where people could feel the magic, allowing themselves to become part of the story, being moved and uplifted by the messages they portray.

Tahlia loved the art form of writing movies, the skill in leading the audience to be moved, inspired, uplifted. Through her writing, she wanted to create a space where the audience would receive messages in a fun way that would genuinely help them through life.

Tahlia wished she could nail a fantastic script, one that would become a mega-hit, radiating a fabulous message, inspiring millions of people. Glancing around at the pressure cooker she was in, her dream seemed hopeless. She knew she had to escape that office grind before it was too late.

Mindlessly walking home, totally exhausted from her own emotions and thoughts, Tahlia knew something in life was missing. She felt bored, trapped, and stuck in a grind of the same old, same old. She craved so much more because an innocence inside her believed that life is supposed to be a magical and fun adventure. What could she do to create this life she knew existed? Tears began to roll down her cheeks as she craved and yearned for so much more.

In her mind, Tahlia saw words flashing in red neon lights, Happiness is a choice! Regardless of what life brings, you get to choose every day. Am I going to be happy or not?"

Tahlia's thoughts became preoccupied with those words for the rest of the walk home. *Could it be that simple? Just choose to be happy.*

Arriving home, Tahlia found herself in a whirlwind to clean up last night's mess. It's like she needed to remove all remnants of her failed suicide. She was surprised at how fast and efficiently she moved. Having emptied the trash and cleared away the final debris, Tahlia looked around satisfied.

After all the emotions that had played out in her day, Tahlia decided she wasn't feeling hungry, so she chose to skip dinner. Instead, Tahlia took a long shower allowing the warm water to stream down her back, feeling a tiny amber of happiness flicker inside her.

Tucked up in her bed, sinking into her fresh sheets and pillow, Tahlia wanted to believe there is so much more to life than suffering, lack, loss, and unworthiness. *There has to be a way forward without the struggle,* she thought. *If only I knew how.*

"What is the way forward?" she whispered into the darkness of the night.

∞ 4 ∞

THE PAIN IN SUICIDE

TAHLIA FOUND HERSELF back in Ivan's quaint house, sitting up on the sofa, facing Ivan, her hands wrapped warmly around the hot chocolate he had made for her.

"Is that better?" Ivan asked.

"Thank you, It's very comforting," replied Tahlia

Tahlia could see a beautiful wooden carved box on the small table next to Ivan's curvaceous cozy armchair where he sat. Ivan's hand hovered above the box, his fingers lightly lowering down to rest gently on it. Tahlia sensed it held something precious, perhaps something that was his daughter's. Ivan's gaze caught Tahlia's eyes, looking at his fingers on the box.

Tahlia had always been a curious child, sometimes blurting things out before thinking, as her curiosity would get the better of her. Now was one of those times where her words came forth without thinking.

"Lovely box, Ivan, is there something precious in there?" As she heard herself speak, she felt foolish. *Wasn't it obvious, Tahlia, can't you ever keep your mouth shut?* She inwardly chastised herself.

Ivan was silent, tracing his fingers along the wooden box, which only made Tahlia feel worse.

"I'm sorry, none of my business, please forgive me. I've always been a little curious." She wished the earth would open up and swallow her, right now.

The corner of Ivan's mouth curled up. "Curiosity is good, Tahlia; it will take you many places. One of the keys to life, I believe, is to follow your curiosity."

Digesting his words of wisdom, Tahlia noticed Ivan's hands pick up the box and draw it close to his heart. He seemed to take a deep breath as if breathing in the essence of the box, and his fingers slowly opened it. Ivan delicately pulled out an envelope, from which he removed a neatly folded piece of paper.

"Tahlia, this is the letter my daughter Madeleine left me; it reminds me every day to live life to the fullest. My curiosity is tugging at me, telling me to read it to you; would you be open to hearing it?"

Tahlia didn't know what to say; she felt it was such a vulnerable thing he was about to share with her, an unknown stranger in his house. She was amazed at Ivan's courage, and something inside Tahlia knew she had to hear it.

"I would be honored for you to share it, Ivan."

Ivan momentarily became lost in his thoughts. Losing Amelie to cancer was difficult. She was such a kind, generous woman, so full of life. Watching her fade away into a thin shell of who she was had been heart-breaking. Ivan still loved her dearly and felt her with him every day. Then losing their daughter Madeleine to suicide had shattered him; if only he could have saved both of them.

The suicide was horrible. Madeleine, in her late teens, appeared happy, although perhaps she never fully recovered from her mother's death even though she was very young when Amelie had passed away. Madeleine was a kind, caring girl, quite sensitive. Ivan thought Madeleine knew that he, her father, loved her dearly. Ivan tried to go out of his way to show her love and make her feel special. He did his best to be both a mother and a father. He worked hard to support them both and ensure that she could be happy. Ivan had noticed that Madeleine was a bit of loner, as she never really appeared to fit in with all her friends. Madeleine tended to spend a lot of time alone; her favorite thing was to be in nature and talk to the plants and animals. She was always saving some little creature.

Ivan allowed these fond memories of his two loves to pass through him. Looking up at Tahlia, her delicate features reminded him of Madeleine.

Ivan cleared his throat and began: "Dear Papa, I love you to the moon and back and always will. I am sorry you are reading this, as it means I am no longer physically with you. Please don't be angry – I had to end my life; I didn't feel I had any other choice. I'm so sorry; please forgive me. I don't know the amount of pain you must be feeling right now but know I am at peace. I am with mamma, and we both send our love." Ivan glanced up to take a sip of water and continued:

"Papa, I was trying to be happy, but everything got too much. All the girls at school are so mean, forever making fun of me. They think I'm spoilt; they have no idea what it is like not having a mother. The pressure of trying to keep the house tidy as well as go to school and get good grades. My life seemed so unfair and those girls they are lucky, but yet so very mean. I feel I'm constantly living in the shadow of others. Whose shadow I don't really know. I didn't feel I could live up to everyone's expectations, especially those I placed on myself. I'm sorry I don't have it in me to become the person I was supposed to be." Ivan paused, reflecting how tortured Madeleine must have felt.

"Father, I didn't want to be a burden on you anymore. I see you pushing yourself to keep a roof over our heads and food on the table, barely existing day to day. I feel a big hole of emptiness inside of you. Papa, you deserve a good happy life, one of fun and joy. I can't stand seeing you sad and lonely." Ivan's voice weakened as he took a breath.

"Perhaps ending my life is the easy way out, please know I have honestly tried my best to fit in, yet I feel so lonely in this world. Papa, it wasn't you, it was the thoughts in my head, you have always been so positive seeing me as your precious child, thank you. I just couldn't understand how life can be a gift when all I see is pain, sadness, and suffering all around. I wished it didn't have to be this way. I wished there was a better way, one where we could be at peace with all the craziness going on in this world. Papa, you were nothing but kind and loving to me; thank you. Please know I am at peace now; no more bullying girls at school, no more thoughts of not being good enough, no more feelings of unworthiness. I am free now. Know I walk beside you, every day, in everything you do. Call on me whenever you need, I will do my best to bring you peace, I love you to the moon and back. Xoxo, Madeleine."

Tahlia had tears streaming down her face as Ivan folded the letter gently, replacing it in the envelope inside the box. He was surprisingly composed, allowing only a small tear to trickle out of the corner of his eye. Tahlia was bewildered at Ivan's composure. *How could he sit there in peace, all the pain he must feel?* Tahlia's tears made her feel vulnerable.

A firm knock on the door shattered the tender moment.

"I'm here," announced a vivacious, robust man, bursting into the lounge room. He grabbed Ivan, giving him a big, affectionate bear hug. The momentum of the embrace pushed the man forward, but he stopped instantly in his tracks as he noticed the young women sitting on Ivan's lounge. His head swung back around to his friend Ivan with a confused look.

"Sorry my friend, did I interrupt something?"

His enthusiasm and curiosity helped Ivan smile and become much lighter.

"Hi, I'm Serge," said the big man, introducing himself to Tahlia.

Tahlia still felt vulnerable; the emotion of Madeleine's letter had been a little too close to home for her. This man, appearing to be full of life, had no idea he had walked into such a sensitive moment.

"Has the cat got your tongue?" nodded Serge inquisitively at Tahlia. "I'm sure you have a voice." He leaned closer to her, "I can see in the depth of your eyes your soul longing to be expressed."

Lost for words, Tahlia thought, *how could he see all this from her eyes?* She wouldn't have picked him to be the deep-thinking type. If anything, Ivan appeared to be the deep thinker; stable, quite distinguished looking. The energy of this new man seemed to be curious, a little rough around the edges, yet fun-loving, an adventurous type.

"Okay, if you're not going to tell me, I'll have to play a game with you," he remarked, pulling a funny face. Serge's energy was infectious. Tahlia started to giggle.

"I'm Tahlia," she smiled, stretching her hand out to shake his.

"Welcome, Tahlia, what brings you here? Ivan never has visitors, except for me," laughed Serge.

Searching for words, Tahlia didn't know how to respond.

Ivan interjected, "I found her on the path, shivering and unconscious."

"Oh, that's you, Ivan, always saving people." Serge was proud of his friend and happy to let Tahlia know it.

"Ivan is a kind soul who always has your back, and if I know him, he would have made you comfortable and warm. No one could have a better friend; he has been my best friend for a million years. Tahlia, you are one lucky girl Ivan found you."

Tahlia could sense how both men seemed to complement each other in a strange, peculiar way. Yes, it was lucky Ivan had found her.

Serge couldn't stand seeing people unhappy and noticed that the energy in the room was rather flat. "You both look like you need some cheering up, let's go for a drive to the beach. It will be fun!"

∞ 5 ∞

A GIFT IN THE STORM

IVAN, SERGE, AND Tahlia were all jammed into a small car, traveling down a windy road. Tahlia noticed everything seemed so colorful, the sky a lovely shade of blue, the grass lush and green. The car pulled up near a small beach surrounded by tall cliffs. It was a beautiful, sunny day – such a contrast to the bleakness she had just been through.

"Come on, let's all go swimming," urged Serge

Tahlia made an excuse; she decided to sit on the shore and watch, as she felt she needed some space; everything was so overwhelming. Tahlia watched the two friends race off into the water, wishing she felt the same joyful enthusiasm for life as Serge did. Instead, Tahlia felt more like Ivan's daughter, caught in despair.

Reclining back onto the beach, doing her best to block everything out, Tahlia drifted off. But then, feeling the sun disappear behind the clouds and a change in temperature, Tahlia opened her eyes to see a massive storm cloud looming above her.

Ivan and Serge nowhere to be seen. *Where were they*, she thought, standing up waving out to sea, expecting to see them. Tahlia noticed the waves were pounding on the shoreline. Big gusts of howling winds brought with it pelting, sideways rain. Tahlia made her way to the water's edge, waving frantically, yelling for Ivan and Serge. There was no sign of them. Tahlia panicked. *Maybe they have drowned.* Her eyes were searching around, trying to see some sign of life. It was hopeless; there was no sign of anyone, not even a soul on the beach. The weather had closed in, Tahlia peered back out to sea. Ivan and Serge had disappeared.

She started walking head-on into the wind, sand, and debris whipping up from the beach, making it hard to see. Tahlia was feeling lost, all alone, forcing herself forward against the howling wind and rain. She became frustrated, her emotions matching the ferocious weather. Tahlia felt hopeless; how would she ever find her way home?

As the rain pelted down, stinging her face, Tahlia was angry with life. Ivan and Serge had probably drowned. How unfair and cruel life seemed, what is this whole process of life about anyway when we only end up dying? The angrier she became pushing forward through the howling wind, the more it seemed to push her backward. Feeling the pressure of everything, Tahlia fell to the sandy beach, pounding her fist.

"I've had enough; I want to go home. I just want to be happy," she screamed into the wind.

Suddenly, the wind and rain seemed to ease, as if they had heard her. In that lull, Tahlia noticed something a small shape, standing in the shallows on the water's edge. Tahlia stood up to move closer. There, standing up amongst the pounding waves, was a little wooden angel. Tahlia was perplexed to see the statue physically standing, how was it possible between the crashing waves and whirling wind? Tahlia couldn't believe it; she looked around suspiciously to see if there was anyone else on the beach, expecting someone had planted it. No, not a soul, the beach was deserted, not even a seagull.

Tahlia leaned down, drawn to touch the statue to see if it was real. Her fingers touched the angel's wooden wings. Tahlia jumped in shock, as she had been sure it was an illusion; another game life was playing on her. Her head was spinning, peering around. Finally convinced no one was playing tricks on her, she picked it up and examined the angel. It was light but felt solid; measuring about the length of her forearm. The angel appeared hand-carved out of some type of dark wood, her body a cherub- shape with beautifully carved feathered wings, delicate ankle and knee creases, a cute round bottom, the angel's hands positioned in prayer at her heart. Tahlia was fascinated by the detail on the angel's chiseled face; eyes, nose, lips, chin, even cheekbones, and hair. Tahlia was in awe, *How exquisite!* She thought. Tahlia had a hunch; the angel was feminine, she felt so precious as if she held an incredible inner beauty reflected in the craftsmanship of her outer beauty. Bringing the angel close to her face, Tahlia looked into her wooden eyes.

"Who do you belong too? Where have you come from?" Inhaling a big sigh, Tahlia drew the cherub angel in close to her heart.

∞ 6 ∞

MYSTERY ANGEL

TAHLIA'S EYES BURST open. Wow, what a dream! Ivan's home, Madeleine's suicide letter, the beach with Ivan and Serge – who were these characters? Everything had felt so real. Lying on her back in her bed, staring up at the ceiling, it took Tahlia a few minutes to pull herself back out of dreamland. She was curious to know what it all meant.

As Tahlia rolled over, she felt something fall off her chest. What was that? Tahlia threw the covers back, and to her utter bewilderment, lying next to her on the bed, was a hand-carved wooden angel, precisely the one she had found in her dream.

"No way," she shrieked aloud. "I was just dreaming; this can't be real." Tahlia touched the angel again, her fingers feeling the solid wood. "Oh, my God!"

Tahlia jumped out of bed, running around to see if any doors or windows were open. Maybe someone had come in last night and planted it there. Perhaps one of her friends was playing a trick on her. In a panic, she went from room to room of her tiny apartment: Zero, Zilch, no sign of entry from anyone, not a trace.

Tahlia raced to the bathroom mirror, looking into her eyes, pinching her cheeks to see if she was real.

"I'm Tahlia; I'm 27 years old. I have a heart-shaped birthmark on my right upper arm." Tahlia hiked up the sleeve of her pajama top, "Yep, it's still there," she confirmed, rubbing her hand on the birthmark.

Tahlia thought, *I am alone, there is no one here, what possibly could explain this?*

"Breathe, Tahlia. Breathe, deep inhale, slow exhale," she heard the words of her yoga teacher soothing her nerves. Convinced she was standing in her bathroom and wasn't going mad, Tahlia tentatively walked back into her bedroom.

There, lying peacefully on her bed, was the mystery wooden angel. Tahlia hesitated before gently picking up the cherub, noticing a few granules of sand caught in the crevices of her bent arms. Holding the angel, Tahlia's hands began to vibrate, sending strange feelings through her.

"Morning, Tahlia, today is going to be a good day."

Startled, dropping the angel, Tahlia realized it was just her phone's alarm going off. Calming herself with her breath, Tahlia switched off the alarm, checking the phone to see what day it was. Friday.

Keeping the angel in her sight at all times, Tahlia quickly got dressed for work; she didn't want any more tricks played on her. Giving herself a quick five-minute makeup session, Tahlia peered into her own blue eyes, noticing they seemed to be sparkling today. *Intriguing,* thought Tahlia, considering what had transpired throughout the week and the huge night she had just experienced, tossing and turning in her dreams.

Tahlia made her way to her dresser, pulling out a silk scarf, one that had been her grandmothers. Gently wrapping the angel in the scarf and placing it in her handbag, Tahlia observed her hands were still vibrating.

Tahlia walked to work for the second day in a row, this time with a vibrant spring in her step, a completely different person from the one who had walked to work yesterday. Tahlia was trying hard to recap her dream from last night, still trying to fit the pieces of the puzzle together. How did Ivan survive Madeleine's suicide? Who was Ivan and Serge, where did they go? How did she end up with the angel? Still not convinced the angel was real, Tahlia thought, *I wonder if Helena will be able to see it physically?* Tahlia reached her hand in her bag, checking to see if the angel was still there. Secretly she was hoping Helena could see it, as she couldn't wait to share it with her.

Tahlia swaggered into work, waltzing past everyone, happy and bright. Raising eyebrows with her dialed-up energy.

Caleb immediately saw how bright and bubbly Tahlia's mood was, an extreme contrast from her attitude over the past six months.

"Wow, what happened to you last night? Mmm, let me think; I bet you got laid." He laughed with certainty and relief. For ages, Caleb had been telling Tahlia she needed a good night in the sack.

"Very funny, Caleb, and wouldn't you like to know," Tahlia replied, leaving him wondering as she raced to Helena's desk.

Tahlia gave Helena a big hug and whispered in her ear, "Have I got something to share with you!"

Helena notice the buoyancy in her friend; it could only mean one thing. Oh, she loved a good juicy story, and this was shaping up to have the makings of one. It had been way too long since Tahlia had a boyfriend or even a one-night stand.

"Let's head to the park at lunch," said Tahlia.

"Aren't you even going to give me a hint, or a name?"

Tahlia raised her index finger to her lips, indicating it was a secret.

"Tahlia, you can't do this to me, what about the first letter of his name," begged Helena.

Zipping her lips closed with her fingers, Tahlia shook her head, patting her handbag as she walked away.

"P.S. – make sure you clear your workload; we may need the whole afternoon," Tahlia called over her shoulder, leaving Helena in suspense.

Tahlia peeked into her handbag, checking the wooden angel was still there, then placed her bag on the desk. She was not letting this angel out of her sight.

Getting straight to work, Tahlia needed a reality check to ensure she wasn't going stark raving mad, plus Tahlia knew she had to get some work done because once she told Helena everything, that would make it all very real and she wasn't sure what would happen next.

Tahlia's hands were still vibrating, her attention focused, breezing through her emails, finding quick solutions to the questions in her inbox. She had three script amendments waiting, and whizzed through them, really enjoying the writing. Tahlia's imagination and creativity were on fire, exactly knowing what needed to be altered and enhanced.

Finished in no time, Tahlia threw the amended scripts down on Caleb's desk. "All done, now I'm going for a long lunch," she said with a smirk.

Caleb was speechless.

Tahlia left the office, grabbing Helena by the arm, "Let's walk and talk."

"I'm dying to hear what happened; you are a different woman today. He must have been incredible!" said Helena, bursting to hear Tahlia's story.

"Let's just say it was one hell of a night!" Tahlia replied, grinning from ear to ear, not quite sure she was ready to reveal the angel to Helena just yet.

Walking fast, Tahlia guided Helena off the pavement into a small charming bookstore. The bookstore was full of crystals, spiritual books, and vast assortments of tarot decks.

"What are we doing here?" Helena asked.

Tahlia was acting strange and somewhat secretive; she had cornered Helena into a little nook in the store and was fumbling in her bag. Looking over her shoulder, Tahlia thrust the wooden angel into Helena's hand. Helena was perplexed.

"What's this?" Helena gazed upon the most exquisitely carved wooden angel she had ever seen. Mesmerized by its beauty, she was speechless.

Finding her voice, Helena asked, "Tahlia, this is exquisite. Where did you get it?"

"Oh, my God, you can see it. It's real, right?" Tahlia was thrilled Helena could see it.

"Um…yeah! It's definitely real," replied Helena, still a little confused.

"Can you feel anything?" asked Tahlia.

"Tahlia, whatever is in my hands, looks like an angel or maybe a cherub. It feels wooden, should I be feeling anything else?"

"No, no, I was just wondering," Tahlia said, reaching out to take it back.

Helena pulled the angel away from Tahlia's reach, "Not so fast, Tahlia, you have more explaining to do."

"Well, that's why we are here. I've booked us an appointment with Madame Lush, the physic," said Tahlia, shrugging.

"Tahlia, why are you acting so weird? You haven't even told me about your night, and now you are dragging me in to see a medium. What in the world is going on?" Helena was holding Tahlia's angel ransom; she wanted answers.

"Okay, in short. You know how I've been feeling pretty depressed and low lately?"

"That's stating the obvious," said Helena.

Tahlia found it hard to say the actual words. "Well, um, two nights ago, I took a lot of pills mixed with a bunch of vodka and tried to suffocate myself in my pillow."

Helena's mouth fell open. "You what? Why? Tahlia, why didn't you say something to me – you know I'm always here for you? What the…?" Helena didn't know whether to be compassionate or angry.

"Helena, I know you are always there for me; the why is not important right now." Tahlia held her hand up as Helena tried to interrupt. "Please, hear me out. Ever since that night, I've been having these strange dreams and visions where I've met this man whose daughter committed suicide. Then last night, I met his friend and we went to the beach, a big storm broke out, and they disappeared. When I woke up, I had this angel lying next to me in my bed." Tahlia stopped for a breath.

Helena grabbed Tahlia by the arm, not entirely following her story, "First you are telling me you tried to kill yourself, and it's not important, then now two random guys you met gave you this angel last night? Tahlia, what the hell is going on?"

Realizing Helena was a little upset with her, Tahlia apologized. "I'm sorry, Helena, for not reaching out; I guess I thought it was normal that we all have suicidal thoughts at times."

Helena interjected abruptly, "Not to the point where we purposely take a cocktail of pills and alcohol, Tahlia."

"I didn't tell you, Helena, because I didn't want to disappoint you." There she had said it, the truth, her fear of disappointing her best friend. "But the good news is I didn't succeed."

"Tahlia, you are my best friend. I love you no matter what, and I'd do anything to help you. Without our friendship, Tahlia, I would be lost." Helena's sincerity showed in her eyes as her tears welled up. Sensing now was not the time or place, Helena pushed her tears back and redirected the conversation. "So, who are these two strange men you keep seeing who gave you the angel?"

"No, Helena, I'm trying to tell you, in my dream, I found the angel on the beach and then when I woke up this morning and the angel miraculously was there, in my bed. I have no idea where she came from, who put it there. It's a complete mystery. I know it sounds crazy, but you know I believe in magic, and you do, too. That's why we are here – to get some answers."

Helena's mind spun, trying to digest everything Tahlia had said, her eyes examining the angel for clues. This wooden angel Helena was holding in her hands was real, but how could it have just shown up? What did the angel have to do with her friend's suicide attempt, and who are these guys Tahlia mentioned?

"Tahlia, Helena, are you ready?" a booming voice sent shivers down Tahlia's spine, followed by an unusually dressed woman.

Madame Lush appeared shamanic in style, dressed in a colorful Peruvian style poncho over a cotton dress, adorned in a necklace made of feathers and jewels, her presence larger than life.

Helena raised her eyebrows at Tahlia, quickly pushing the wooden angel back in Tahlia's hands, as Madame Lush ushered them into a small, dimly lit room.

The room filled with crystals, scattered around the room, large ones strategically placed in each corner forming a grid. Candles flickered on the bookshelves alongside statues of deities, sage sticks, and tarot decks. In the middle of the room was a small round table holding a Himalayan salt lamp and a few smaller crystals. Tahlia noticed that under the table was a massive rose quartz crystal. *This vibrant woman certainly had an infinity with crystals*, thought Tahlia.

Madame Lush showed them to an old, plush velvet lounge, as she sat behind the little round table with the salt lamp.

"How can I help you?" Her voice was commanding.

Tahlia held up the cherub angel, "Can you tell me where this comes from?"

"Heaven," smirked Madame Lush as she rolled her eyes.

"No, seriously, it mysteriously showed up in my bed this morning I had been dreaming that I found it on the beach and when I woke up it was in my bed." Tahlia was searching for an answer.

"Sounds like to me someone has been astral traveling," Madame Lush said as she reached out to take the angel.

Tahlia gave Helena a look of "Help me!"

Madame Lush held the cherub angel in her hands, examining it, trying to get a feel for it, making strange faces as if she was picking up some physic information. "The only thing I am picking up is that it is a gift for Tahlia. Which one of you is Tahlia?" she announced powerfully.

"Me," said Tahlia.

Madame Lush leaned in towards Tahlia's face. "I see, you have been in a very dark place of late, lots of extremely dark thoughts, leading you to the point of giving up."

Tahlia interrupted her. "Yeah, yeah, I know that, but I'm not here for a reading on me and my dark thoughts. I want to know about this mystery angel, and we don't have much time, I'm sure there is lots to tell me."

"Very well, but be mindful of your thoughts," said Madame Lush quite firmly, as she sank further back in her chair. "This angel, it's a gift for you, Tahlia."

"Who from?" asked Tahlia.

Both she and Helena looked on, hoping for an answer.

Madame Lush ran her hands over the wooden cherub. "Nope, no answer on that, but it's not from around here."

Madame Lush continued to feel the angel, tracing her fingers slowly along its torso.

"She is powerful and crafted with such exquisite inner beauty, full of feminine energy oozing out of her. There's something magical she wants to share with you."

Madame Lush closed her eyes, her eyelids flickering as if she were getting a clear message. Tahlia and Helena looked on in anticipation.

"She is very precious, Tahlia, a gift that in time you will unravel. You are to ensure you take good care of her. Keep her close." With that, Madame Lush opened her eyes and handed the angel back to Tahlia.

"That's it?" asked Tahlia.

"Yes. Thank you, that will be $40," Madame Lush held out her hand.

"You can't be serious; there has to be some other message. What's the magic she wants to share?" Tahlia asked, desperately seeking clarity.

"That's not for me to say." Madame Lush hesitated, "Wait, hang on, I think there may be love coming soon."

"You think," scoffed a disappointed Tahlia as they walked out.

Walking down the street, Helena was still mentally piecing it all together.

"What do you think, Helena?" asked a distraught Tahlia, hoping her friend might know.

"Tahlia, I'm upset to hear you tried to take your life; you know you mean the world to me. As for your visions with these strange guys, well, you've always had strange visions. However, this angel, she is so mysterious. Maybe your guides have crafted this and sent it to you to help you out of your sadness and despair. I can't explain how it showed up; does it even matter? I believe it's a magical gift for you. Maybe a beautiful reminder of the magic of life."

Tahlia thought for a moment. *Yes, the magic of life, hadn't her grandfather always taught her that life was full of magical moments?* As a child, Tahlia loved to write and create fantasy worlds all the time in her imagination. It all started from sitting around the fire with her grandfather, whom she had loved dearly. He had died when she was young, but fond memories of him always came flooding in. He was a gentle soul who loved the land and Mother Nature, often talking to Tahlia about the magic of life. He would assure her anything is possible if you put your focus and intention on it. Tahlia loved being with him, as he was the only one who seemed to understand; they were kindred spirits. Her grandfather talked about following your bliss, but she had no idea what he meant back then, and had decided she was supposed to follow your curiosity. That is how she became so interested in the mystical, quantum physics, and the healing arts.

Tahlia wished he was still here with her. Would he be proud of whom she had become, the women she had grown into? Tahlia realized that Helena and herself were kindred spirits too, in that same way, always doing the best to find the magic in life, following their curiosity. Tahlia loved this about Helena and their friendship. No matter where the experience of life led them, she knew that Helena would always have her back, believing in the mystical and magical. It was a special bond they shared.

Helena disrupted Tahlia's train of thought, "No point heading back to the office. Before we left, I marked us both as having a meeting on location this afternoon. Let's say I had a hunch that this afternoon would be interesting."

The corner of Tahlia's mouth turned up as her hand fondly rested against the angel in her bag.

"Tahlia, I don't believe that you need to take your mystery cherub angel to any more psychics. I believe you have to let her magic surprise and delight you. Because one thing I know for certain is that you are a completely different woman today, your enthusiasm for life has returned, and I am so thankful for this angel that I still have my friend here with me. Promise me you'll never get to that point in life again and not reach out to me. I am always here for you, no matter how dark your thoughts may be."

"I promise," Tahlia smiled, both friends embracing in a big hug.

Helena was right, no more mediums. Tahlia needed to follow her curiosity, trusting her heart to lead her to wherever she needed to go.

"Now don't forget to pack tonight, our flight to Hawaii is tomorrow afternoon," waved Helena as she dropped Tahlia off.

Hawaii! Shit, Tahlia had utterly forgotten that Helena had organized a well-needed get-away for them. Previously consumed in her dark thoughts, the thought of going on a vacation had not even enthused Tahlia. Thank goodness, Helena had a sixth sense that Tahlia needed to escape.

"Tahlia, maybe you should bring the cherub angel," nudged Helena. "Let's see what magic she helps unfold for us."

∞ 7 ∞

A VISION

TAHLIA PACKED LIGHTLY, leaving room for her wooden angel, wrapping the angel in her grandmother's scarf to protect her. Tahlia's mind was still boggling over everything that had transpired.

Ever since her failed suicide attempt, Tahlia's life had become so mysterious. All those dreams, alluring eyes, free-falling, meeting of Ivan and Serge, strange visions she still couldn't piece together. So much had transpired over the previous week that Tahlia was relieved to be escaping and getting away. Perhaps it would all start to make sense once she got out of her environment. Tahlia loved traveling and always returned home with a fresh new perspective on life. Yes, this was just what she needed.

Helena was as much a travel addict as Tahlia, and both embraced the opportunities that allowed them to adventure and spend time together as friends. Helena knew Tahlia had been fragile over the last few months but had no idea she was in such a dark place. Secretly, Helena was thrilled the mystery angel had showed up. What would she do without her best friend?

Excited, they found their seats on the plane, heading for the Big Island of Hawaii, a place of magical beauty and fun.

Tahlia carefully tucked her backpack under the seat in front of her. At the last minute, she had a thought to pack the angel in her on-board bag rather than check it in her luggage. She wasn't sure where that thought came from but followed her instincts. Careful not to put her feet on it, Tahlia settled in. The week had taken a toll on her. As soon as the plane was at cruising altitude, she felt herself starting to nod off.

"Tahlia, Tahlia," she heard her name whispered. Those alluring blue eyes once again staring back at her. *Oh no,* thought Tahlia, *last time I fell!* Tahlia found herself backing away, toppling into a massive hole. She somersaulted backward, over and over, not knowing which way was up, nothing stopping her fall, the bottom of the earth sucking her through into an endless void. Tahlia kept falling, twirling, and spinning; she became nauseated. *I think I'm going to throw up,* she thought, blacking out.

When she came to, Tahlia noticed she was floating, perched on some kind of transparent wings that felt soft and reassuring. This feeling was familiar, yet she had no idea where she was or who she was. It was as if her whole identity – everything to this point that had defined her – was now stripped away. Instead, she felt like a clean slate, a person she didn't even recognize. There was an expansive feeling of exquisite joy in her heart and an enthusiasm for life beyond her imagining, something she had not felt for a very, very long time.

The graceful presence that had caught Tahlia began to hum sweetly to her. Tahlia could feel the vibrations of the humming going right through her. The sound of the hum was consistent, following an ebb and flow to a soothing, sweet melody.

"Who are you? Can I see you?" Tahlia asked inquisitively.

The presence formed into a beautiful ethereal woman standing in front of Tahlia. Her light was bright white, her energy exuding pure love. Tahlia was breath-taken by her exquisite beauty.

"I'm Seraphina," she said softly, "I've been watching you for a while now."

Something in Tahlia nudged her to ask, "Did you give me that wooden angel?"

Seraphina's beautiful presence smiled at her, "Sort of." Her voice seemed to hum the words when she spoke.

"Your cherub angel is a gift, a reminder of your inner beauty. You can always feel the connection to your true essence vibrating within that angel, divinely supporting and guiding you."

Tahlia thought of the strange tingling feeling she had felt a few times when she was holding the wooden angel.

"Your cherub holds within her vibrations of exquisite joy and awe, the magic of life. Every time you look at her or hold her, she will radiate exquisite joy back to you. Tahlia, your wooden angel will help you remember your intention to radiate joy into the world."

"What do you mean, my intention?" asked Tahlia, unsure when she had decided this.

"Your birth intention is what some people call your North Star. When birthed into this physical world, all souls have an intention. Tahlia, you chose to come here to radiate exquisite joy in everything you do, while manifesting a life you love."

Tahlia had heard of one's North Star but had never envisaged it as her soul's intention.

"Tahlia, you will discover this intention of vibrating joy; seeing all through the eyes of wonderment is what you will leave as your life's legacy. You will show people how to do this. It is your gift to the world."

"My gift to the world, but how am I meant to do this?" Tahlia's mind and fears were stepping in.

Seraphina placed her hand on Tahlia's head as if to soothe her rampant thoughts. "All will be revealed in time. Trust, this is so. Life is a journey, Tahlia, always remember it's not about finding joy; it's about radiating and vibrating joy. The feeling of joy will attract wonderful things to you."

As magically as she had appeared, Seraphina disappeared.

Tahlia had so many more questions, what was she supposed to do now with this gift? Would the wooden angel show her? Tahlia could feel her hands tingling, her entire body vibrating. The humming was still resounding and pulsating waves of joy and happiness through her.

"Tahlia, Tahlia, fasten your seat belt." Helena's hand was gently shaking Tahlia awake. "We're about to land."

Tahlia looked out the window to a vision of lush green tropical scenery. It was the Big Island of Hawaii surrounded by beautiful aqua blue water. Tahlia looked at her hands as they continued to vibrate gently.

Helena and Tahlia unpacked in their hotel room, both full of excitement. Helena knew how much Tahlia needed this and couldn't wait to see the magic they created together as friends. Tahlia welcomed the time to chill out and relax, knowing she and Helena would have fun. They always did.

"Look at that magical view, how good is this going to be?" exclaimed Helena.

Tahlia was unwrapping her mystery angel, not sure whether to say anything to Helena about her vision on the plane.

Peering over Tahlia's shoulder, Helena asked, "Have you got a name for her?"

Tahlia looked at the angel and looked up at Helena, "I think I'll call her Seraphina."

Helena smiled, "Seraphina, what a fitting name for such a mystery angel."

Tahlia placed Seraphina on her pillow.

∞ 8 ∞

EXQUISITE JOY

HELENA AND TAHLIA grabbed their beach gear and headed off. They found a secluded beach, complete with a lifeguard tower. The water on the waves glistened like diamonds, beckoning them in. Setting up their towels and deck chairs, snorkels in hand, Helena and Tahlia headed into the glittering water.

They swam over to a little reef shelf, exploring. The water was so clear you could see every little detail: unusual coral, unique shells perched on the shelf of the reef ledge, tiny fish swimming in and out. Helena and Tahlia were in heaven, Tahlia could feel all her worries melt away into the water.

Watching from the tower, the lifeguard was smiling at how happy those friends seemed. He loved seeing people enjoy the ocean, as he believed it was such a magical place. The beach could relieve so much tension and bring joy to many. He loved that everyday nature brought with it something different: dolphins, whales, turtles, big waves, small waves – such a playground of fun. Through his binoculars, he spotted a big old turtle hunting for food along the reef shelf. He waited to see if the girls noticed it.

"Tahlia, look," motioned Helena, pointing toward the turtle.

Wow, how big and majestic! Tahlia observed its well-formed shell and was surprised at the turtle's agility and speed in the water. *Aren't turtles meant to be slow?* She shrugged off her thought.

Helena was thrilled. She had always loved turtles; having read somewhere they represented feminine energy and were closely connected to Mother Earth. Helena snorkeled behind, following the turtle.

Tahlia continued exploring, focusing on the reef fish darting in and out of the coral. All of a sudden, a large pod of dolphins came swimming up beneath Tahlia, so close she could almost touch them. About forty of them, rising from the depths of the ocean floor, spinning around in the water. The dolphins were swimming on their backs, looking Tahlia directly in the eye. Tahlia's heart instantly burst open, tears streaming down her cheeks, flowing into the water. As the tears flowed, her heart opened wider, transcending all her ugly thoughts and feelings about herself and life. It was as if the dolphins were magically releasing her heart, caressing away all her troubles. Tahlia felt her chest expanding like a balloon, filling up with love and joy. Tahlia immersed herself entirely in her surroundings, being aware of the crystal-clear water rippling in the sunlight as the dolphins played around her, under her, above her. Time stood still; the only thing that mattered was this exquisite joy she felt in her heart. Tahlia had never experienced anything so beautiful yet powerful. She could sense the dolphins resonating a thought wave towards her; *play, have fun, life is so worth living*. Tahlia promised herself this magical experience would forever be etched into her heart and soul, the feelings of fun and exquisite joy impregnated into her being.

Eventually, the dolphins swam on, and Tahlia looked around to see Helena, who had followed the turtle. She, too, had spotted the dolphins and was elated.

The girls headed back to the beach. *What an incredible start to the vacation,* thought Tahlia filled with immense gratitude for her friendship with Helena and the magic they always seemed to attract.

The lifeguard watched as the girls stepped back onshore, invigorated and excited, their smiles beaming across the beach.

He noticed something different about these two friends; they shared some kind of mysterious, even magical, quality.

"How cool was that Tahlia, you have to love Mother Nature," remarked Helena.

Still radiating with joy, Tahlia agreed.

"Now it's time to get some sunshine on this white body," laughed Helena as she wriggled herself into a comfortable position on the beach chair.

Tahlia was more than ready to surrender to the warming sun, penetrating its rays into her. *Ahh, a place of total surrender*, she thought, as she just let go, melting into the chair, feeling her skin tingling and vibrating.

Tahlia's curiosity and sensitivity seemed to have been heightened by the experience with the dolphins. *What is happening? I have no idea who I am anymore*, thought Tahlia. She could feel her whole skin vibrating, coming alive, every cell of her body radiating and feeling incredible joy. She noticed how fantastic she now felt, such a contrast to the person she had been over the past few months.

Tahlia drifted off, seeing herself in her bed the night of her suicide attempt; she still felt ashamed of her actions that night. Imagine – if she had succeeded, she would have missed the most amazing experience of her life, swimming with the dolphins. She would not know this incredible feeling of connection and love. Tahlia's heart was open and full; she found it hard to comprehend that she had been that low, to a place where she felt there was no other way.

She flashed to a vision of Ivan and how distraught Madeleine's suicide must have left him. Guilt washed over Tahlia as she envisioned how her own family would have felt. Perhaps they would have blamed themselves, too, thinking they were not enough. Helena would have been utterly devastated. Tahlia knew for sure she never wanted to inflict that type of pain on anyone.

As she let go and drifted further into another time and space, she found herself once again on those transparent wings, floating from mountain top, to mountain top, drifting way down into the valleys, but never hitting the valley floors. It was like with every descent she was lifted back up just before she hit rock bottom.

Surrendering into this marvelous feeling, Tahlia floated through the scenes unfolding in front of her, smiling from ear to ear, realizing how much she loved life and was in total awe.

As she embraced the journey, Tahlia began to notice that some scenes were delightful and fun, other scenes were stormy and heavy, reminding her of some of her roller-coaster emotions. Particularly that time in high school when the girls were bullying and teasing her, saying she was useless and selfish, telling her she wasn't good enough to be part of their group. That had deeply hurt Tahlia. Yet this time, it was as if Tahlia were hovering above the scene, witnessing her younger self, the traumas that had taken place, or at least what Tahlia had felt were traumatic, all while still being able to feel this exquisite joy and sense of wonderment. Looking at everything through different eyes, Tahlia came to see a lost, lonely, scared little girl inside each of those bullying girls, projecting their pain onto Tahlia. Tahlia found that instead of reacting to their hurtful words, she could feel compassion for them, acceptance that allowed her to feel joy.

Floating from scene to scene, Tahlia was able to maintain her sense of peace by vibrating joy. Observing and being in the moment, she felt safe, allowing it to unfold with no fear or expectations, just compassion, awe, and appreciation. Tahlia felt an expansion of joy in each moment regardless.

As the sparkling sun warming her skin seemed to dim, Tahlia could feel herself slowly opening her eyes, teetering between her vision and lying on this sunny beach in Hawaii.

It was his energy she felt at first, drawing her toward him. Tahlia blinked her eyes and noticed this rather buff, cut, lifeguard walking toward Helena and her. She couldn't put her finger on it, this feeling she had felt before. Tahlia dismissed it as perhaps she was still tripping from her vision.

He swaggered over, Tahlia noting that the lifeguard exuded a certain sense of assurance.

"Sorry to disturb you, ladies."

Helena woke from her nap.

"I noticed that you have been lying here for over an hour and a half without anything to drink." He handed them both a bottle of water.

"Thanks," the girls replied in unison, not able to take their eyes off him.

As Tahlia reached for the bottle, her hand touched his; it sent tingles down her spine. Pulling away, she looked over at Helena, who seemed quite pleased with his thoughtfulness and appearance. Helena was besotted, her eyes tracing his buffed olive skin, to his extremely fit torso, leading up to sun-kissed brown hair where a pair of Maui Jim sunglasses framed his face.

"I noticed you got to snorkel with Tessie, the old sea turtle," he said, making small talk.

"You've named her?" said Helena sitting upright. "How gorgeous, she must be so old."

"Yeah, she has been coming to this reef forever. Tessie's over fifty years old. My father used to snorkel with her when he was young."

"Wow!" Helena was fascinated, engaging him in the conversation.

"It's one of the best things about my job. I love it when the dolphins, whales, or turtles turn up. It's like the animals know which people need inspiring, and a bit of joy sprinkled into them that day. I love seeing the smiles of delight on people's faces," he rambled.

Tahlia smiled to herself, precisely what she had needed, some hope that life can be magical. Tahlia looked on, sipping her water, a little transfixed by the magnetizing energy she was feeling.

The lifeguard raised his sunglasses. "By the way, I'm Mike, your local lifeguard."

Tahlia was stunned. Staring at her were those alluring blue eyes she had kept seeing of late, the ones originally from the marketplace in her vision.

Helena reached out to shake Mike's hand, "Helena and Tahlia," she replied, pointing to Tahlia.

Mike and Tahlia's eyes interlocked, both momentarily mesmerized and enchanted.

Mike cleared his throat, breaking the awkward moment, "Okay, ladies, I've got to get back to the tower, duty calls. If you need anything, let me know. By the way, be mindful of how much sun you are getting, it can be a little strong on the Big Island, even as beautiful as she is."

Mike turned and walked casually back to his tower.

Rattled by her recognition, Tahlia said, "Helena, that guy; I recognize his eyes. I've seen them before; I don't know where, but I know those eyes!"

"Of course, you do Tahlia, he is so ridiculously cute, why wouldn't you think you know him – or at least wish you knew him," Helena laughed.

"No, seriously, I recognize those eyes from one or more of my 'traveling visions,'" she said, raising her fingers in quotations marks. "You know, in my mind."

"Oh, right. Yes, Tahlia, your 'visons' – it must be an omen." She jokingly mocked Tahlia.

"All I know, Mike is super cute and thoughtful. Maybe a little fling would be just what you need. I saw him staring back at you."

Tahlia couldn't believe Helena was mocking her.

Helena had started to pack up. "Regardless, I think Mike is right, and we've probably had enough sun for the day, let's head back into town."

The girls gathered their things, Mike waving to them as they left. Both girls walked off with a spring in their steps.

∞ 9 ∞

ALLURING EYES

HELENA AND TAHLIA had freshened up, and the sun was setting as they wandered through the local streets, coming across a cute little café, with an outside garden bar, overlooking the water.

"I think this is perfect for a sunset cocktail or two," announced Helena. "Shall we?"

Tahlia and Helena shared a friendly smile as they entered the bar, finding the perfect spot to sit to share the sunset. Sipping on Mai-Tai's, relaxed, and enjoying the ambiance, the two friends shared some fun memories, laughing and smiling.

Helena was quite animated, discussing Mike. "How cute was that lifeguard? Those chiseled abs on his fit tanned body. What a superb vision to wake up to on the beach, wouldn't it be funny if we ran into him again?"

Right on cue, Mike sauntered into the restaurant, with an adorable, well-behaved golden retriever beside him.

"Aloha, Kimo," Mike waved at the Hawaiian bar attendant.

As he began approaching the counter, Mike couldn't help but feel a familiar energy radiating from one of the tables. Mike turned his gaze to the right, noticing Tahlia and Helena, and immediately diverted toward their table.

"Fancy meeting you here," Mike said, nervously patting his dog.

Helena almost choked, spraying her Mai-Tai everywhere. Tahlia's heart skipped a beat, her body tingling all over.

"Would you like to join us?" Helena said, winking at Tahlia as she quickly wiped up her mess.

"Thanks, but no thanks, I mean not for long, I'm just here to grab a takeaway," Mike was a little flustered, his gaze landing on Tahlia.

Helena noticed Mike's dog wagging his tail, "Boy or girl?"

"This is Max, and last I checked, definitely a boy."

Everyone laughed, breaking the awkwardness.

Max went to Tahlia, giving her a nudge with his wet nose; she patted his soft, shiny coat as he sat beside her, loving the attention.

"Max seems friendly," Tahlia said softly.

Mike gazed at her tantalizing eyes, and Tahlia once again was mesmerized. The intensity of his gaze made her blush even redder than she had become from the day's sun.

Mike diverted his gaze to Max, patting him affectionately on the head. "Yes, this old boy is a good friend. He lives with my Ma and Pa. They don't live too far from here."

"So, you live here?" questioned Helena.

"Only temporarily during the summer. I come back home to help my parents out, as they are getting old and I love lifeguarding at the beach during the day. Plus, it's always a good reason to come back and spend some time with my pal Max." Mike was ruffling Max's coat.

Max returned the affection, wagging his tail, staring back at Mike with his big brown puppy-dog eyes.

Tahlia noticed how affectionate Mike was to the dog and caught herself thinking, *Mike must be a nice guy with a kind soul.* Tahlia reprimanded herself, *who could tell for sure, from two brief meetings?*

"Where do you live, then?" asked Helena.

"In California, Santa Monica."

Helena kicked Tahlia's foot under the table as if to say, can you believe that?

Tahlia couldn't look at Helena as she knew she would laugh.

"We both live in Santa Monica, too, what a small world," said Helena.

Their conversation was interrupted by the bartender.

"Here's your takeaway, Mike." Kimo handed Mike a calico environmental bag, simultaneously patting Max, who wanted to nuzzle into the food. "Not for you fella, I'm sure Mike's got something yummy for you at home."

"Ladies, another drink?" said Kimo as he cleared their glasses, wiping the table.

Being a lover of cocktails, Helena couldn't help but say, "Yes, please, what is your specialty?"

Kimo looked at Mike, and they both exchanged a cheeky smile. "Two Lava Flow specialties coming right up." Kimo grinned as he strolled back to the bar with their empty glasses.

"Sorry ladies, I have to head back home, mum and dad are waiting for dinner." Mike bent down, encouraging Max to come, having a hard time getting Max to leave Tahlia's side.

"Looks like someone is fond of you," said Mike, looking at Tahlia. She blushed again.

"Nice talking with you both. I'm sure I'll see you again," said Mike, turning to leave.

Looking over his shoulder, directing his gaze at Tahlia, "Enjoy the Lava Flow cocktails; Kimo makes a mean brew." Mike smiled as he and Max disappeared.

Tahlia knew for sure they would catch up again. She couldn't explain this inner knowing; she just had that sense. What Tahlia didn't realize was just how soon it would be.

That night Tahlia couldn't sleep and found herself wandering the beach under a shining full moon. Up ahead, she could make out a figure coming toward her. A sudden burst of tingles drew Tahlia's attention toward the pit of her stomach. Looking down, placing her right hand on her stomach Tahlia questioned herself. Was her intuition warning her of danger, or was it the same magnetizing feeling she had felt each time she saw those alluring eyes, the same eyes Mike had? As Tahlia lifted her head, she almost collided with Mike.

"Hey, there," remarked Mike, "three times in one day, I must be a lucky man."

Tahlia blushed; thankfully, it was dark, and he couldn't see how flushed her skin had become.

"I couldn't sleep, thought I'd take a walk and find some inner peace," she said nervously.

Mike couldn't help but notice how this woman filled him with a sense of intrigue. His body would tingle around her; there was something about this woman that drew him to her. Tahlia couldn't deny the attraction she felt for him and wondered if Mike felt the same.

"You're shivering; here, put this on," he said, gently placing his soft sheer, long-sleeved white shirt over her shoulders.

"Thank you," she whispered, allowing his gentle touch to linger.

They wandered the beach talking about the stars, the moon, nature, the magic of life. A flickering spark of connection grew; it seemed their souls were dancing together with every conversation. Reaching the sandy path leading to Tahlia's accommodation, Tahlia went to hand Mike his shirt.

"No, you keep it for tonight." He gently put his hands on her arms, drawing her body close to his.

Tahlia felt safe and nurtured in his embrace. The vibration of energy electrified between them. Mike leaned in to kiss her, and as he did, Tahlia responded. It was a soft, gentle kiss, full of promise, lighting up every cell of her body. Their mouths were connecting, exploring, lingering in the moment.

Mike gracefully pulled away, holding her hands. "I've had a wonderful night talking with you, Tahlia. Thank you." He dragged himself away from her gaze, turning and walking into the darkness.

Bringing her fingers to her mouth, Tahlia traced where his lips had been. Her lips were tingling, vibrating with a feeling she had felt before, but not sure where.

∞ 10 ∞

SYNCHRONICITY

HELENA, ALREADY DRESSED for the days' adventure, noticed a man's sheer white shirt draped over the chair. As Tahlia came out of the bathroom, Helena held it up, "Excuse me, where did this come from?"

Still trying to make sense of what had happened last night and not ready to ruin the magic, Tahlia laughed it off. "Oh, that, we can talk about it over breakfast," she said, looking around, grabbing her bag as she walked out the door.

Sitting at the beach café, Helena prompted Tahlia, "Okay, I'm dying to know, where did that shirt come from? I know I drank a few extra Mai Tai's last night, but I don't remember seeing or hearing any men here last night," said Helena, rubbing her head.

Tahlia replied casually, "I may have gone for a late-night beach walk, and I may have run into Mike."

"What the...How is that even possible?" Helena was confused.

"I honestly don't know," said Tahlia. "I guess it's magical. Maybe it has something to do with the angel. All I know is a lot of things have been a bit strange since I found her. I keep getting these odd, familiar feelings."

Helena agreed as she had noticed a few unexplained things happening.

"So, tell me, you ran into Mike on the beach, at night purely out of the blue."

"Yes, exactly. I couldn't sleep, so I went for a walk to get some peace in my thoughts, and we practically ran into each other." Saying it out loud, Tahlia herself found it bizarre.

Helena's eyes opened wide in awe of the magic unfolding for Tahlia.

"We walked and talked, enjoying a fabulous lovely conversation."

"And…anything juicy to share?"

"I was cold, so he gave me his shirt."

"Hang on, girlfriend; you're telling me he was shirtless again. Oh, my," exclaimed Helena with a big grin, fanning herself. The thought of Mike shirtless was enough to get Helena's hormones and energy rising.

"Sorry to disappoint your fantasy, my friend," Tahlia replied. "He had a white T-shirt under his shirt. You know, the whole layering fashion thing."

"Oh, what a shame for you. I hope it was a fitted white T-shirt," Helena said, smirking.

"Yes. All right, Mike looked pretty damn sexy," Tahlia surprised herself with her answer.

"Anyway, he walked me to the sandy path, I went to give him the shirt back, and instead he leaned in and he kissed me."

There it was. Out loud. Tahlia hoped that this was true and wasn't another one of those visions.

Helena was thrilled, "I bet he is an amazing kisser! What was it like?"

Tahlia's lips began to tingle, she could still feel the soft touch of his mouth, exploring hers, and she smiled.

Helena threw her arms up, rubbing her hands together. "Say no more, Tahlia, the look on your face is enough to tell me it was sensational!" she shrieked.

***

Tahlia had wished for a sign in life that would make her feel excited again. That vacation was where it all began, their destiny sealed.

Mike and Tahlia's relationship moved very fast; everything seemed to have a natural flow. Not to mention this unique sensation Tahlia felt every time Mike touched her, nothing she had experienced before with past boyfriends. It was like sparks of lightning pulsating throughout her whole body, even when he held her hand. She knew that sensation was familiar yet couldn't put her finger on it.

Mike had fun showing both Tahlia and Helena some of his favorite spots on the Big Island, with Max always accompanying them. Mike and Tahlia formed a deep connection in the magical hours they spent together.

Tahlia noted all the coincidences; Mike was only temporarily living in Hawaii for a few months in the summer. For the rest of the year, he worked at Disney as a creative in the Art Department, the same industry as Tahlia. As it turned out, Mike's home in Santa Monica was only a few blocks from hers. Mike and Tahlia had lots in common, including some friends. Tahlia was secretly excited by all this synchronicity.

Helena was over the moon that Tahlia had met someone; at last, she could be happy. Happiness was all Helena had ever wanted for her friend. She was hoping this would be what made Tahlia bounce back into life and leave behind her lost, depressed state.

∞ 11 ∞

THE SNOWBALL OF LOVE

BACK AT HOME in Santa Monica as their relationship continued to grow, Tahlia knew this man would walk beside her through life. He was an adventurous soul, kind-hearted, and loads of fun. Mike captivated her, his kind caring eyes inviting her to be far more than she could imagine to be. She had seen these same alluring eyes in the marketplace in her unconscious suicidal state. Could his eyes be beckoning her into a new life? Where would this journey lead who knows, but all she could do was go with the flow.

Mike felt invigorated and fulfilled when with Tahlia. He enjoyed her belief in the magic of life and loved her crazy different perspectives on life. She shared his adventurous and spontaneous way of life. He felt happy when he was with her and knew she would be the perfect partner for his journey in life.

Like a snowball rolling down a hill gathering high-speed momentum, it wasn't long before Tahlia and Mike accepted that they were destined to be together and moved into an apartment. They eloped in a small ceremony, as neither wanted a big wedding. Tahlia and Mike celebrated their romantic union in the pristine waters of Hawaii, being married on paddleboards off Kahaluu-Keauhou Bay on the Kona Coast of the Big Island.

Mike and Tahlia began a new chapter of life together as husband and wife.

Exploring, hiking in the mountains, Mike doubling Tahlia on his motorbike, cruising through pretty valleys. Days spent swimming, paddle-boarding, water skiing, as Mike loved boats and the ocean. They were having fun, traveling, and adventuring together. Mike and Tahlia's friends could see the strong connection and depth of love they shared. Life was flowing brilliantly.

After being married for only eight months, Tahlia found herself pregnant. "This is a good thing, right?" she asked Mike, hoping to reassure herself.

Mike was super enthused, nodding his head and hugging her, "It's fantastic, Tahlia!" Tahlia was apprehensive, fearful of this significant life change. She felt anxious; what would that change look like?

After the first scan, Dr. Lewis looked at Tahlia and Mike, "Congratulations, it's twins."

"What? No, the scan, it must be a mistake," said Tahlia.

Dr. Lewis reassured them, "The scan shows two little embryos, indicating it most definitely is twins."

Tahlia was beside herself, thrown into panic.

Mike was grinning, taking it all in, "What's wrong, Tahlia? Twins is exciting, maybe it will be one of each, a boy and a girl, all at once."

Not convinced, Tahlia threw her hands up in disbelief. Her thoughts were running rampant: *How on earth am I going to handle two babies at once? No, this can't be happening.*

Lying in bed that night staring into the darkness of the night, Mike sleeping soundly next to her, Tahlia was anxious, thoughts swarming through her head. She rolled over toward her bedside table and fumbled for her mystery wooden angel. Everything in life had been flowing so incredibly well. Tahlia had never felt so joyful, and now all of a sudden, the news of expecting twins triggered Tahlia, putting her in a spin. Her thoughts were spiraling out of control, all her old insecurities of not being good enough flooding like chemicals into her brain taking over her body.

"Please help me. I'm scared; I don't know how I will cope. What happened to the joy I was feeling? Please, somebody, help me." Tahlia's desperate plea was vibrating across the universe.

Her angel felt and heard Tahlia's cry for help....

Tahlia saw herself sitting all alone in a dark forest. Coming toward her was a familiar presence – Seraphina. Tahlia recognized her beauty and grace. As Seraphina moved closer, Tahlia could hear a gentle hum as her body began to vibrate.

Seraphina's presence appeared so pure, such a contrast to Tahlia's.

It had been some time since she had spoken with Seraphina. Swept up in the romance with Mike, Tahlia had forgotten about Seraphina.

"Tahlia," whispered Seraphina, "follow me."

Seraphina led Tahlia farther into the forest, continuing to hum, not saying anything, walking her through a door in the trunk of a gigantic tree.

Tahlia found herself in Ivan's house once again. Ivan and Serge were sitting, laughing with each other.

"Oh, my, look who has showed up," Serge greeted Tahlia with a big bear hug.

Ivan was smiling, "Welcome Tahlia, would you like something to drink? I'll get you some of my special hot chocolate." Ivan made his way into the kitchen.

Tahlia was ecstatic; she hadn't seen Ivan and Serge since that day on the beach. They were still here, they hadn't drowned as she had thought when she found the mystery angel.

"What can we do for you Tahlia, you look so concerned, in fact frightened," commented Serge.

Tahlia spewed all her concerns out, "I'm so glad you are alive. What a relief I thought you had drowned."

Serge looked a little confused.

"A lot has happened since last I saw you. Life has been full of adventure and fun. I met a lovely man named Mike. We are married, I love him, he is wonderful, but now I'm pregnant with twins. I'm so worried that I'm not ready for this journey. I don't even feel good enough to be a mother. All my insecurities have reared their ugly heads. I don't know how I will cope."

"I think you need more than a hot chocolate," Serge said, patting the sofa, indicating for her to take a seat.

"Tahlia," he said, holding her hand, "one thing I know for certain is that the only guarantee in life is change. Look around at nature; it's constantly changing every day."

"But Serge, I was so happy things were going so well, I was in a much better place. You would think the news that I am having a baby, two babies, would make me feel excited. Instead, my head is swarming with fears and anxiety, old horrible thoughts swarming around again, I don't understand."

"This's normal, Tahlia; your brain is full of all your past experiences, and they get triggered."

"How come I wasn't triggered when I was joyful and having so much fun in the moment? Now I'm worried about the future, and all those thoughts have come flooding back."

"Exactly, Tahlia, when you were in the moment, focusing on joy, you felt wonderful, didn't you?"

"Yes," Tahlia said, a little skeptical, trying to see where this was going.

Serge continued, "Things were a little bit out of your control, but you were able to go with the flow because it was exciting, and love was what you wanted."

Tahlia answered with a slow, hesitant, "Yeah."

"Now all of a sudden, something is in front of you that you didn't expect or want. Your brain picks up the signals that things are not okay, not to your liking. It wants to protect you, keep you safe and comfortable. The only way your mind knows how to keep you safe is by controlling your future based on your past experiences."

Tahlia looked a little dazed, trying to comprehend Serge's words.

"Tahlia, our past patterns will always try to control the future when we are triggered. When something new is in front of us, and it's not familiar, our brain doesn't have an experience of it, so it doesn't know what to do. Hence, it tries to control things from past experiences, telling you this is uncomfortable, focusing you on fear, not joy, and expansion."

Tahlia took a big breath, processing his words; she certainly could feel all the fear.

"Life is magical, Tahlia, every moment delivering you something new and different, an opportunity to grow. Our role is being able to show up, to witness what is unfolding in front of us. Allowing it to be, observing all your concerns floating up and through, without judging, resisting, or latching onto them. Each moment brings an opportunity for you to decide to flow with what's unfolding. You get to choose to go with the flow happily with ease and grace, or you can choose to struggle and resist, creating suffering and misery. It's your choice, Tahlia."

Tahlia's mind shot back to the dream she had on the plane to Hawaii. A vision of sitting on those transparent wings that seemed to carry her from mountain top to mountain top, avoiding the valley floors, through all those scenes, good or bad. She remembered the ability to look upon those situations through the eyes of compassion with the intense feeling of joy, no matter what.

"Does that mean I need to find joy in every moment?" queried Tahlia.

"No, not exactly. Tahlia, every situation and moment are just experiences, regardless of our likes or dislikes. Sometimes, we look at situations in our life, and it feels impossible to find joy because our brain won't comprehend, this is just an experience. Instead, it tries to control us through our past experiences, telling us how unfair life is, life shouldn't be this way; this is not what we wanted." Serge paused, waiting to see if Tahlia was following. She acknowledged with a nod.

"Tahlia, the magic lies in Accepting; this is what it is. Surrendering, allowing yourself to feel joy regardless and to see the beauty in every moment. Joy then becomes the vibrating signal you are emanating, and you become a magnet, attracting more joy. Even though the situation still is not how you would have liked it, you can flow through it with inner peace. Inspiration will begin to appear, and you will be surprised at how easily things unfold." Serge paused, taking a sip of water.

"I like to see it as a choice, accepting the moment, vibrating joy from my heart regardless of the situation! Tahlia, this is the magic of life." Serge was smiling, his energy beaming.

Tahlia felt herself being pulled out of her dream, Serge's smiling face drifting into a thin vapor as she felt Mike nuzzling into her, kissing her good morning.

"Morning, my mother-to-be," he said, affectionately rubbing her tummy. Tahlia struggled to bring her awareness back to their bed, Serge's words ringing in her ears. Tahlia glanced down and noticed she was hugging her wooden angel at her heart.

∞ 12 ∞

SEVEN YEARS LATER

TAHLIA AND MIKE journeyed through the birth of the twins and all its changes, everyday life settling into a constant groove.

Jayden was a happy little boy, just like his dad, giggling and laughing, always creating with his hands. He shared Mike's passion for boats and a love of the water. Jayden was happiest in his own company and uncannily connected to nature, reminding Tahlia of her grandfather.

Sierra was a compassionate, sensitive soul, appearing shy at first yet very social and loving toward her friends. She had the wildest imagination and was always coming to Tahlia with fabulous stories, often mentioning how the angels were continually guiding her. Sierra didn't like doing anything unless she asked her angels first.

Caught in the vortex of doing, Tahlia realized that life has a strange way of getting away from you, the years sneak up without warning. The toddler years had whizzed past; the twins were seven now and well into school. Tahlia found it had been life-changing, a massive juggling act between caring for the twins, married life, and her career. Tahlia likened her life to a circus performance, juggling many plates in the air, hoping she could catch them all.

Life went on day after day with its constant demands, Tahlia never really knowing how the plates would land. She often threw caution to the wind and hoped for the best. Like that time the twin's day-care rang Mike when Tahlia had forgotten to pick up the twins and had gone for a massage instead. For some reason, she had completely forgotten it was her day to pick up the kids. Tahlia never lived the guilt of that day down. She had forgotten to catch the plates that day; in fact, they smashed on the floor, shattering, leaving a shard of glass in her foot, always reminding her of her guilt.

Mike was a caring and kind father; he was good with the kids, always doing the best he could around the demands of his job.

Mike and Tahlia's relationship was still loving and fun, yet both of them often seemed a little frayed at the edges. It wasn't the perfect family life Tahlia had dreamed of. She had come to settle with their life; perhaps her lofty ideas were not reality. Even so, Tahlia could never shake off the feeling that something seemed missing.

∞ 13 ∞
LIFE'S DEMANDS

LIFE SEEMED QUITE hectic, always somewhere to go, something to do. It was like a whirling vortex sucking Tahlia in with no way out. Yes, she loved the twins and the joy they brought Mike and herself, yet the struggle was real. As the vortex kept spinning, Tahlia's enthusiasm and vitality for life seemed to have swirled out of her grasp.

This morning, Jayden and Sierra were up chasing each other around the house, Mike was ready to head off to work, kissing her good-bye, leaving his dirty plate on the bench. Tahlia wandered around in a daze, picking up the plate, loading the dishwasher, brushing Sierra's hair, all on autopilot. Whose life had this become? Going through the motions, Tahlia loaded the twins in the car, dropped them off at school, finally venturing to work herself. She was grateful it was Friday and that they would be heading off to Hawaii on a family vacation.

Driving to work in the same old traffic, Tahlia became aware no one seemed happy in the cars near her. Most people either had a look of worry or exhaustion etched on their faces. Some were talking on their phones, quite animated, trying to squeeze in a conversation before they reached their destination.

Stopping at the traffic lights, peering around at the other drivers, Tahlia couldn't help but wonder, *Do they feel the same as me, trapped and bored with the mundane? Are they craving more fun and adventure, some kind of peace, or joy?* She sighed. *How did we all become so trapped in who we thought we should be? Grow up, get a job, marry, have kids, and just do life. There has to be more to life; this couldn't be all there is!*

"What happened to all my dreams, those fun travel adventures, the lightness and sense of awe I used to feel? Where has the innocent beauty of life gone?" Tahlia heard herself voicing these questions out loud, thumping her hand on the steering wheel in frustration. "There has to be a more fulfilling way! What can I do to create a life I love?"

Tahlia carried this air of agitation with her as she moved through the office, bumping into work colleagues whispering gossip and negativity to each other by the coffee machine. Not impressed, she shot them a look of disapproval; she hated gossip, as it always involved putting someone down. On the way to her desk, Tahlia observed other staff staring blankly into space or with their heads buried in their computers, probably already facing the dreaded email loop.

As Tahlia settled into her desk, she consumed herself with the scripts in front of her, hearing a voice echo:

"Life is supposed to be fun; it's a choice. Show up, bring joy to each moment, regardless! Tahlia, this is the magic of life."

Tahlia's body was tingling with goosebumps, the ones that felt like truth bumps. Where did this voice come from? Her brain was searching for where she may have had heard or even read this. Was it even possible to bring joy to each moment?

Tahlia fell quickly into a vision; her whole body was tingling and vibrating. She saw herself as a little girl, in awe of all the beauty in the world full of enthusiasm. She remembered having so much fun and playing with life. Making up stories, talking with cows and goats on her grandparents' farm. She was so innocently loving life and could see the beauty in everything, even the "ugly" things. Tahlia could feel how she wanted to tell the whole world that everything radiated beauty and life is playful and fun.

Suddenly fear crept in. What would people say, would they think she was crazy? No one in her family seemed to see what she saw; her friends couldn't even understand her joy for life.

In her state of observing, this tingling, joyful vibration seemed to be racing through her entire body being projected into all her fears, soothing them. Tahlia could feel the joy without even thinking about it. This joy seemed to be part of who she was; it appeared embedded in her body. Best of all, this tingling joy was able to override ugly, fearful, not-good-enough thoughts, and behaviors. Tahlia surrendered to the process, feeling the joy, seeing the inner beauty in life.

She mumbled to the universe, "I love this joyful feeling, this sense of inner beauty, I want to keep expanding it. Please universe, if I can have this joyful feeling forever in every situation, I promise I will inspire others, showing them how to feel this for themselves, inspiring them to uplift their lives."

"What will you show others, Tahlia?" Helena interrupted, standing at Tahlia's desk, pausing as she noticed Tahlia's face seemed to be glowing.

"Me? Oh, nothing," Tahlia replied, trying to compose herself.

Helena shrugged, "Okay, whatever you say. Are you ready for lunch?"

"Yeah, hang on a second," Tahlia fumbled for her bag, her brain scrambling to get it all together.

Walking down the crowded street, Tahlia could sense an air of unhappiness, seeing stress upon people's faces. How could she relate this incredible feeling of joy to them? How could she inspire them to be uplifted and manifest a life they love?

"Tahlia, are you are okay?" Helena probed, "you've got this weird glow about you."

"Have I? Really? No, I'm all good," she said, adjusting her posture as if nothing were different. Tahlia wasn't sure how to explain this vision to Helena. Did Helena see it as well, all the stress on people's faces; could she sense the underlying unhappiness?

Wondering what Tahlia was hiding, Helena choose to ignore it. "Sushi good for you?" Helena asked.

Tahlia nodded as they stepped into Mr. Wong's.

As they ate lunch, Tahlia was consumed with thoughts about Helena: *Was she truly happy, had she manifested a life she loved? I mean, on the outside, Helena appeared to have it all together. She was very successful in her career, happily married to Leo, with one child, a boy, Jake, whom they both adored.*

In between sushi rolls, Tahlia summoned up the courage to ask, "Helena, are you truly happy? Do you feel you are in love with your life?"

Helena pondered for a moment; Tahlia felt a dark cloud hover above Helena's head.

"I would say aspects of it I love; I love my family and friendships. I love nature." She paused, Tahlia sensing the dark cloud becoming bigger.

"Am I in love with my life? Honestly, Tahlia, no. My life seems to be on autopilot, every day going through the motions. I wished I didn't have to work full time. I would love more time to be creative, to paint, to cook, to go camping on weekends with Leo and Jake, without having to worry about getting all the washing and food shopping done and being ready for the workweek. I would even love a chance to contribute at Jake's school, read or help out with art projects, you know, something that would fulfill me." She took a breath, "I just feel that we are always trying to catch up, chasing the money, there is either no time or money for the things I love."

Wow, that was a big download, totally unexpected, no wonder Tahlia had sensed a dark cloud.

Feeling the sadness in Helena's heart, Tahlia asked, "Would you say you've lost your spark for life?"

"It's not lost, it just feels rather dim at present, while I am getting by and trying to make the best of things."

Tahlia wanted to help her friend change her sadness.

"Helena, what if I told you that you able to feel joy in all areas of your life? Joy truly is there, you can tap into it, your life can be fun regardless of its demands," added Tahlia enthusiastically.

"Tahlia, look around, it seems every day comes with it demands, no one has enough time to add joy to their life, we are all busy trying to survive."

Tahlia was a little surprised that Helena was so cynical.

"I agree we seem trapped in a vortex of surviving, but what if there was a way we didn't have to just focus on surviving. If there was a way to move through life and its demands, happily, with ease and grace."

"Tahlia, you have always been a dreamer, wanting people to be happy."

"But Helena, so have you, when did we stop dreaming?"

"Haven't we all stopped dreaming?" Helena paused, looking up at Tahlia, on the verge of tears.

"Helena, I just had a vision at my desk. I saw that we are not our thoughts, nor are we what is happening to us. Everything is a creation; it all has its unique beauty. Helena, I could see the energy inside our bodies, all of us vibrating joy, with our thoughts floating by not getting stuck or pulling us down. We can bring joy into everything, even the ugliest situations. I saw how life is supposed to be light and fun; we get to choose; it's easy." Tahlia was on an excited rant.

Helena intercepted her, "Let me get this straight, I'm not my thoughts? They are just bubbles of energy floating by, and I am a joyful tingling in my body, no matter what happens to me?"

"Yeah, that's it!" shrieked Tahlia.

"Tahlia, when those doubts and fears wake me up in the middle of the night, they are real. Real concerns about money, Jake's health, our life. I lie there staring at the ceiling for hours, trapped in worry and fear; there is absolutely no joy floating around in those moments."

"But Helena, the joy is there, it doesn't have to be 'found.'" Tahlia continued, trying desperately to prove it to Helena. "What is your worst fear?"

"Being broke and homeless, nowhere for my family to live, no food to feed them."

Tahlia was stunned how quickly Helena had responded. Pausing for a moment, Tahlia decided to take another tactic.

"Okay, obviously this is troubling you. Helena. Let's just imagine for a moment that you are homeless but happy."

"Tahlia, I'd be anything but happy, I would be devastated and stressed."

"Bear with me Helena, imagine being homeless you had no demands of being anywhere, there was a soup kitchen close by to eat at, free showers in the hall. At night you sleep under the bridge by the pier snuggled up to Leo and Jake. The best view in town, watching the waves roll in."

"Look, Tahlia, I see what you are doing. You're trying to make me grateful for something in that scenario. It's not working, and I don't understand where this is going."

"Helena, it's not about being grateful. For sure, that helps, but I saw it more as a sense of freedom in accepting any situation, allowing it to be what it is, without expectations."

Tahlia's body kept vibrating, tingling with joy, fueling her with enthusiasm, she couldn't understand why Helena wasn't comprehending this.

"What if, as life unfolds, we surrender into whatever is in front of us at each moment. Not demanding life to fit into our personal likes or dislikes, not resisting, not clinging, instead simply surrendering with an inner knowing, trusting that this or something better is coming our way? In that knowing, we could feel joy and make different choices. We could come up with creative solutions."

Helena stood up, pushing her chair away from the table "Tahlia, I can't get into the vibe of your fantasy right now. Leo and I had a big fight over money last night, and I'm not feeling any joy." She abruptly walked out.

Horrified she had been so preoccupied with her own excitement of the vision, Tahlia realized she hadn't even seen the signs of how unhappy Helena was. Embarrassed, she got up following her friend.

"Helena, is there anything I can do?"

"No, Tahlia, I'm sure we will work it out, things are just a little tight right now. All I want is to give up work or go part-time, and I can't because we need the money."

Tahlia could feel Helena was on the verge of tears but was holding back. Tahlia put her hand on her friend's back, hoping she could transfer some of this tingling joy that was still pulsating within her.

They walked back to the office in silence, Helena was grateful for Tahlia's sensitivity in not probing any further.

Back at her desk, Tahlia's thoughts were running wild. *I expected Helena would understand. I had no idea Helena was troubled about money; she and Leo always seemed to be good.* Tahlia began to think about how disconnected she had become and started to beat up on herself for not sensing her friend's unhappiness. Disappointed in herself, Tahlia noticed that the tingling feeling of joy in her body had dissipated.

Tahlia shook her head as if to clear the not-good-enough thoughts and lonely feeling that had overtaken her. *What can I do to inspire people that this harmony and joy are real,* thought Tahlia?

As she began work on the script in front of her, Tahlia got a flash of insight; *this disappointed, lonely feeling isn't who I am. The disappointment is those thoughts and feelings that surfaced when I expected Helena to understand. When my expectations are not met, these not-good-enough feelings and thoughts appear.* Tahlia could see precisely when her energy changed. *How fascinating,* she acknowledged, *all because my expectations were not met.*

What if I accepted that Helena wasn't in the right mindset and needed more proof? What if I could appreciate this is how it was supposed to unfold? Perhaps there is more for me to learn to be able to explain this concept more clearly. Tahlia's new thoughts were uplifting her. Instantly she began to feel her whole body vibrating again, tingling with joy. Tahlia felt expanded and happy, remembering her declaration to the universe. If I can have this feeling forever, I will inspire others to manifest a life they love. Tahlia knew she had to keep moving with this and explore it some more.

Interrupting her, Caleb arrived at Tahlia's desk, handing her notes and a script. "The film set needs these amendments finalized before you leave today."

"Okay, I'll give it my best." Tahlia shrugged, concerned that she had a lot to complete before she left tonight for their family vacation.

Reminding herself that she is not her fear or lack, turning her attention back to her joyful state, Tahlia placed her fingers on the keyboard and started creating the amendments. Her fingers were typing at a speed she never thought possible, the words flying onto the pages. Some creative force appeared to have possessed her. She felt happy and was enjoying the process. Tahlia even started humming to herself; she was in the flow and loving it.

Tahlia completed the amendments plus the others she had been trying to get through with ease. She even had time to clean her desk before she left for vacation.

Helena gave Tahlia a big hug. "Have an awesome adventure Tahlia, say hi to Mike and the twins. You know I love you no matter how crazy your ideas are at times, I'm sorry I was short with you."

"No, I'm sorry, I had no idea you had money concerns. I honestly meant it; if there is anything, I can do for you, please let me know." Tahlia looked at Helena, "Promise."

"I promise," said Helena. "It was just a silly argument with Leo; I shouldn't have let it get to me."

Tahlia gave her friend another hug, "I love you, Helena."

Helena smiled, "Thanks, my friend, now have yourself a fabulous vacation."

Tahlia waved goodbye as she jumped into her car, appreciating her friendship with Helena. She turned on her favorite tunes, driving home excited that they would be going on a family vacation, and she would have time to explore this new feeling and insights.

***

Walking in the door, Tahlia stopped as she witnessed how happy and peaceful everyone was. Mike had the kids bathed and fed; they were all sitting at the table, laughing. What a different scene from the morning rush, where she had left in a fluster, upset with the monotony of their lives.

Mike was very good at moving through life in harmony with things, as he didn't have the same controlling tendencies Tahlia had at times. Mike seemed quiet and accepting; maybe he knew about this joy thing she had experienced at work. She would ask him later. Tahlia moved in and gave them all a big warm hug and kiss.

Tahlia was tucking Jayden and Sierra in bed, as both twins still slept in the same room.

Excited, Sierra said, "Mummy, do you know that my angels say anything is possible?"

Tahlia smiled as she fondly remembered her angels telling her the same things.

"Don't be silly, Sierra," Jayden butted in, "not everything is possible. Mummy couldn't be an astronaut."

Tahlia laughed.

Sierra bantered back to Jayden, "If my angels tell me it is so, then it is. I know it's true because they show me all the time." Sierra waved her favorite fairy angel around, "See, they even look real."

Jayden laughed mockingly, throwing her a brotherly look like, "You're crazy."

"Sierra, would your real angel like to take a ride on my high-speed boat?" Jayden said sarcastically, holding up his favorite remote-controlled boat.

"Depends how fast it can go," Sierra said, rolling her eyes.

Tahlia interjected before the banter got out of hand, "Okay, you pair, time for sleep, we have an early start for our big Hawaiian adventure in the morning. Good-night, my angels; sweet dreams."

She kissed them both on the checks, smiling at their brotherly-sisterly love; it was cute.

Walking away, it occurred to Tahlia that it had been years since she had held a conversation with her angel Seraphina. Tahlia hadn't dreamt since the twins were born, none of those crazy free-falling dreams where she was transported into a different time and space, another world, Ivan and Serge. What had happened? Was the magic gone? Tahlia felt a wave of frustration with herself; she was obsessed with being a good mum, doing it all right. Feeling totally out of control with the frantic pace and demands of life, she had forgotten her connection with the things that she adored as a child, the magic of life, the very thing that had given her hope. Tahlia could feel a void in her heart as if something were missing.

All those insights at work today, that buzzing feeling of joy, Sierra's excitement and belief in angels prompted Tahlia to think, were they all signs? It seemed rather strange; two reminders in one day, maybe it was time to reconnect?

Tahlia sank into their comfortable bed. Mike was already in bed, on his laptop, looking through the internet at his favorite thing, boats.

Tahlia gazed at Mike, recalling those alluring eyes, the eyes that had nudged her off the cliff, a faint reminder of her failed suicide attempt from all those years ago. The same eyes that had seemed to rescue her. Mike had turned out to be a good man, Tahlia's rock and guiding star. She was so grateful for him in her life.

"Mike, do you believe in magic, that we can experience joy in every moment?"

Mike paused, searching on the net, looking up at Tahlia. Was now the right time to have this conversation? She looked exhausted.

Mike responded affectionately brushing the hair away from Tahlia's face, "A good question, honey, but let's have this conversation on our vacation, you look like you need a good rest." He gave her a loving kiss good-night.

Tahlia was humbled in that moment by his sensitivity toward her. Mike was right; she did need a good night's sleep; she needed to reset. Hawaii was coming at the right time, just when she felt utterly exhausted from the demands of everyday life, realizing she had forgotten what was important to her. Tahlia, fed up with focusing on surviving, wanted to start living, to feel happy, full of vitality, experiencing the magic in life again.

"I know there is a better way to do life; show me how," she found herself whispering.

As Tahlia was falling into a slumber, her grandfather's face popped into her mind. "Tahlia, your soul loves to play and have fun. Allow yourself to be present, accepting each moment, following your curiosity with joy, embracing this magical journey called life."

∞ 14 ∞

THERE IS A BETTER WAY

"RISE AND SHINE everyone, vacation time!" said Mike.

Where had she heard those words before? Tahlia thought as she opened her eyes.

My grandfather, that's right. Dressed in his khaki overalls, Tahlia's grandfather would sit on her bed in the morning, tickling her awake, saying, "Rise and shine, sunshine. What wonderful magical things will we co-create today?"

Tahlia had many fond memories of her grandfather; this, by far, was one of her favorites. She loved seeing what wonderful magical things she and her grandfather would co-create together. They always found the magic in every day. Tahlia had forgotten this little morning ritual that she so loved.

Hang on. Wasn't pop there last night as I fell asleep? Tahlia smiled to herself, noticing the coincidence.

Everyone quickly got ready, full of excitement for their Hawaiian adventure. Tahlia made the last-minute checks, ensuring they had everything. Noticing her angel, Tahlia decided to grab it at the last minute, wrapping it in her grandmother's soft silk scarf, popping it into her backpack. Scurrying out the door to catch their flight, Tahlia was overwhelmed by a strange heavy feeling; dismissing it, though, she closed the door behind her.

The family settled in on the plane. Tahlia sighed in relief, thankful they made it, she so needed this vacation. As the aircraft started cruising at altitude, Tahlia let go, closing her eyes, drifting off into a deeply relaxed state.

Tahlia felt time and space collapse, floating into a peaceful void.

Seraphina appeared, her graceful etheric presence floating next to Tahlia, whispering, "There is a better way Tahlia, you can find joy in everything. Take a breath and know life is always unfolding exactly how it is supposed to be."

Gently Seraphina took Tahlia by the hand and pulled her into a vaguely familiar world. Tahlia remembered visiting this world as a child, where she saw pain and joy as one. In the suffering and struggle, there appeared to be freedom and flow; even though they were opposites, they seemed to co-exist. As Seraphina and Tahlia floated, Tahlia looked closer and witnessed how every negative emotion seemed to climb up a scale, gradually moving into a more positive feeling. Tahlia observed sadness rising up, forming into fear and worry, fear turning into frustration and anger. Anger transcending into courage; courage moved up into acceptance and hope; acceptance leading to love and joy. It was like notes on a piano all existing together, yet every emotion was resounding a different vibration.

Tahlia didn't know why Seraphina was showing her this, but she was mesmerized by this scale. Each emotion played a different note sending out a vibration that would attract those like it. Sadness was a deep low note, vibrating at a low level that attracted more sadness. Love echoed at a high, uplifting level, attracting more love. Tahlia observed how thoughts of sadness could pull you out of the feeling of love. The more she thought sad thoughts, Tahlia could feel her energy lower. Tahlia resisted trying to raise her energy.

Seraphina whispered, "Surrender, accept the feeling, then allow yourself to change your thoughts."

Tahlia let go, sinking into the low vibration. Within that sadness, she began to feel a sense of freedom, and with this freedom, Tahlia started redirecting her thoughts by asking, "What can I do to feel love?"

Tahlia's sadness moved into frustration. "I don't want to be frustrated; what can I do to feel happy?" Tahlia took a long inhale, surrendering, and accepting the frustration. As she exhaled, Tahlia released her expectations and noticed the frustration fade into courage. Inspired, Tahlia asked, "What can I do to feel more joy?"

Instantly Tahlia's courage became a feeling of peace. Within that peaceful state, Tahlia noticed her heart pulsing with joy, the same joyful essence she had felt yesterday in her vision at work.

"Tahlia, use this scale wisely; it will help you manifest a life you love." Seraphina's smooth voice penetrated through Tahlia's body as she disappeared, leaving Tahlia full of questions.

What could Seraphina mean by this? Why me, why was she showing me this? I'm not sure what to do!

Tahlia felt something touching her leg.

"Honey, we are landing," said Mike leaning on Tahlia's leg, planting a kiss on her cheek.

Tahlia opened her eyes and looked down in her lap. She was holding her wooden angel. *That's strange,* she thought, *I don't remember getting my angel out. How did it get on my lap?*

Tahlia looked at the wooden angel, carved so exquisitely. Glancing out the plane window lost in her thoughts, *mystery angel, these visions, how do all these things fit together? There's still so much unexplained.*

Mike's parents' house was not far from the beach where Mike and Tahlia had initially met. Max, the golden retriever, was quite old now, but still greeted them all, wagging his tail. The kids screamed with excitement to see their grandparents and being kissed affectionately by Max.

Mike and Tahlia enjoyed a refreshing drink, sitting on the lanai, talking with his parents as the sun set, throwing colors of orange and red throughout the sky. Jayden and Sierra played in the back yard, Max chasing them gleefully. Looking out, watching the kids playing happily, Tahlia felt a sense of relief roll off her shoulders. Their vacation was going to be a fabulous time away.

∞ 15 ∞

A JAR OF HAPPY MEMORIES

IT WAS A new day: the twins were eating breakfast with their grandparents, with Max waiting patiently at their feet for any crumbs to drop. Jayden and Sierra were mesmerized, as grandpa was playing a magic trick, making a coin appear from behind their ears. Taking in the smiles on everyone's faces, Tahlia took a breath, marveling at how the simplest things can bring so much joy.

Mike came up behind her and snuggled in, kissing Tahlia on the neck. "Isn't it nice to have some family time?"

Tahlia found her shoulders relaxing, a smile in her heart, as she leaned back into him.

"Yes, exactly what we need."

"Are we going to the beach today?" piped up Jayden, running to his mum and dad.

"We sure are," said Mike scooping Jayden up in his arms for a big hug.

"Yay," shouted Sierra, "let's go!"

Mike and Tahlia had often talked about swimming with the dolphins at this beach, and the twins were pumped with excitement to see what the day would bring.

***

Mike was playing with the kids on the beach; they had dug a big hole that Mike was sitting in, and the twins were covering him with sand. Tahlia relaxed, sinking into her beach towel; her thoughts drifting in and out of faded memories. This beach held so many memories for her, swimming with the dolphins with Helena, something she had needed when she was at the lowest point in her life. Those alluring eyes, meeting Mike, all those chance meetings of running into him. The vision and conversation with Ivan and Serge, her mysterious angel. She couldn't help but wonder how or even if all these visons and joy fitted together.

"Mum check it out, dad is now a merman," laughed Jayden. His voice rang right through Tahlia, reminding her of Serge's jovial energy.

Mike was buried entirely, only his head sticking out, with a mermaid's tail made of sand at his feet. Tahlia smiled at how creative and joyful the twins were, loving that they were having fun, engrossed in the moment.

Pretending to be asleep, Mike opened his eyes, exploding out of his sand covering, grabbing the twins, and tickling them. Hysterical waves of laughter filled the beach.

"Who's coming swimming?" said Mike, running toward the waves. Jayden chased after him.

Tahlia noticed Sierra didn't go. She seemed deep in thought, rubbing her hands in the sand.

Tahlia got up and walked over to Sierra, "Is everything okay, beautiful?" Tahlia asked as she sat down on the sand next to her daughter.

"Mum, when we get back home, do I have to keep going to school?"

Tahlia was a little shocked, as this seemed to have come right out of the blue.

"I don't like those bullying girls, they make fun of me, always teasing," said Sierra. "I feel like I don't fit in."

Tahlia had no idea her daughter hated school.

Momentarily, Tahlia became transported back to the girls bullying her on the bus: "You'll never become anything. We don't want you in our group; you're not good enough."

Tahlia could feel how soul-destroying those horrible words had felt. Tahlia didn't want Sierra to be feeling the same and realized this was her chance to change the memory.

Taking a deep breath, Tahlia directed her intention to feel joy in that memory; it wasn't easy, especially as she saw the pain on her daughter's face. Tahlia began seeing all those girls as broken little girls wanting love.

Reaching a place of acceptance, Tahlia asked Sierra, "Honey, tell me something about school that you love?"

"Nothing Mum, it's boring, I hate having to sit in class all day, and the girls are horrible."

"Okay, I see that's what you don't like; can you tell me something you do love about school," prompted Tahlia.

"Well, I guess I love playing outdoor games, and when we get to do fun, creative stuff."

"How does that make you feel when you are playing the games or being creative?"

"I feel happy. It's like nothing else matters." Sierra's eyes were sparkling.

"Wonderful, Sierra now close your eyes. Imagine you have a big glass jar, then paint on it a pretty picture, maybe a butterfly and flowers."

Tahlia could see the corner of Sierra's mouth curl up into a smile.

"Once you have a pretty picture painted on the jar, imagine putting in all those happy feelings. Feelings of fun times with Max, Jayden, dad, me. Your favorite times with grandpa and grandma. Things that make you smile, happy memories."

"Even my angels, mum?" Sierra opened one eye.

"Yes, now keep your eyes closed," encouraged Tahlia. "Here comes a happy memory, quick, catch it and pop it in your jar, and another and another. Is your jar full, Sierra?"

"Almost, there is a little room left," she happily played along.

"Good," said Tahlia, "that means there is always room for more happy memories to put in your jar. Now take that jar and hold it close to your heart."

Sierra moved her hands toward her heart.

"Can you feel it at your heart?" Tahlia placed her hand on her daughter's hands.

Sierra nodded, still with her eyes closed.

"Imagine placing that jar inside your heart, with all those happy feelings. Your pretty jar will always in your heart, and you can ask it to bring you those happy feelings whenever you need them. Now imagine those bullying girls, but keep hanging onto your jar, your happy feelings. Do you think that your happy jar can help you can feel happy no matter what the girls say to you?"

Sierra takes a deep breath, "I'm not sure, mum."

"Sierra, what would your angels say at this moment?"

"They say to open the jar," Sierra eagerly replied.

"Go on, then, open your jar and tell me what happens."

"Mum, I see those happy feelings flying out, making circles around the girls, turning their mean words into big white puffy clouds that float away. Then those happy feelings fly back into my jar. It's like magic. I feel tingles in my body." Sierra opened her eyes wide, all excited.

"Mum, it works, I felt happy, no matter what those girls said. All their ugly words just disappeared."

Tahlia was ecstatic that her daughter was able to have this experience, even if it was in her imagination.

"Sierra, you always have this jar of happy feelings in your heart," said Tahlia, giving Sierra a big kiss and cuddle. It was a lovely moment of connection between mother and daughter, Tahlia simultaneously sensing the healing of her own wounded memories.

Sierra happier now, jumped up, "Mum, let's go swimming with Jayden and dad."

Tahlia and Sierra raced to the water's edge and joined the boys, diving in and out of the waves, playing, laughing as a family. Like magic, they suddenly found themselves surrounded by a large pod of dolphins playing around them. Tahlia was thrilled, hearing the twins shriek with excitement, Mike beaming with smiles, the dolphins surfing the waves, jumping, and spinning out of the water. The twins mimicked the dolphins, trying to catch the same waves.

Tahlia vividly recalled her first experience swimming with the dolphins on the trip with Helena. All the love and joy the dolphins had brought her. Tahlia could still summon up that memory and the feeling of exquisite joy anytime at will, and it was just as powerful and beautiful as when it physically happened. Putting her hands to her heart, offering a thank you to the dolphins and Mother Earth, Tahlia was so grateful to be sharing such a magical moment with her family.

That night they all enjoyed a lovely family dinner filled with laughter and joy, chatting about their incredible day swimming with the dolphins. Mike's parents grinned as the twins showed them how the dolphins were jumping and spinning in the air. Mike laughed, trying to keep Max from jumping up with them. Tahlia enjoyed seeing Jayden and Sierra sparkling-with- joy.

Climbing into bed that night, Tahlia felt so in love with life. *What an incredible day at the beach. Life-changing*, she thought.

Mike noticed how transformed Tahlia's disposition was.

"I love it when you are this happy and relaxed. Before we came away, you seemed worried and stressed, and I don't like seeing you unhappy." He leaned in, hugging her. "Did you still need to talk about joy and the magic of life?"

Tahlia wasn't expecting Mike to have remembered.

"Oh, I guess I was wondering, Mike, do you believe that we can experience joy in every moment?"

"After a day like today, totally," he replied, smiling at his wife.

Tahlia decided at that moment not to say anything more. It had been such a wonderful day; everyone's spirits were high; she wanted them both to savor this good feeling and not ruin it with words. Tahlia smiled at Mike, giving him a passionate kiss as she snuggled into her hubby, enjoying his body next to hers.

∞ 16 ∞

UNEXPECTED CHANGE

THE NEXT DAY was rainy and wet. Mike took Tahlia and the twins for a drive, wanting to show them his local waterfall, cascading into the rock pools. He thought the twins would enjoy an adventure in the rain.

Usually, Tahlia enjoyed the rain and often found it refreshing, but today the rain seemed like such a huge contrast, washing away all the magic of yesterday.

Tahlia found herself thinking about the vision she had experienced in her office before she left. The one where there was joy in every moment. She gazed out the car window, reflecting on her mystery angel, trying to piece it all together. Was her imagination really that crazy, or were these messages? She listened to the chatter of the twins in the back seat.

BOOM! Suddenly their car was screeching, spinning round and round out of control. Tahlia screamed, uncertain where the tailspin was taking them.

A big white truck had come out of nowhere, smashing into the backside of their car, almost splitting it in half. Mike's head slammed into the steering wheel, knocking him unconscious. Tahlia felt rigid and stiff and couldn't move. Desperately trying to take a breath and keep herself conscious, she summoned up the energy to turn around, her eyes catching sight of Jayden and Sierra lying lifeless in the back seat.

Tahlia let out an ear-piercing scream "NOOOOOOOOOOO!!" She tried to reach her hand toward them, but she couldn't move. Tahlia blacked out.

The twins, bathed in brilliant white light, looking serene and graceful, appeared in front of Tahlia. Tahlia motioned to move toward them, wanting to scoop Jayden and Sierra into her arms.

Placing her hand on Tahlia, Seraphina stopped Tahlia from moving forward. "Now is not your time. Tahlia. Jayden and Sierra are safe; we shall take good care of them."

"No, no, let me go. I want my twins." Tahlia anxiously tried to force her way past Seraphina.

The image of the twins started to blur; she heard Seraphina's voice: "Tahlia, your husband needs you; Life needs you."

"No, Seraphina, I need my twins," screamed Tahlia, desperately trying to reach out for her beloved children. It was no use; Tahlia was frozen solid, her arms wouldn't move.

Watching as the pure white light engulfed the twins, Tahlia saw Jayden and Sierra's sweet little faces, blowing her kisses. "Mummy, we love you; we love daddy, too. Thanks for loving us, please stay with daddy, he needs you."

The twins snuggled into each other, happy and serene, fading into the brilliant light.

Tahlia awoke on the ambulance gurney; she was being wheeled into a room full of commotion, lights flashing in her eyes, machines beeping, paramedics telling hospital staff, "It is a miracle she is okay. All organs are intact; there doesn't appear to be any broken bones, only some heavy bruising. She was unconscious for a while. The man, we are assuming her husband, is stable, yet still unconscious, he will need stitches in his head wound. Considering the accident these pair were in, they are lucky. Someone up there was definitely taking care of them."

Tahlia tried to roll her head over to see Mike, her eyes registering him lying on the gurney beside her blood smeared across his face.

Tahlia closed her eyes again as a vision of Ivan flashed into her head, "I know what it is like to lose everything. It is harrowing."

Tahlia's heart shattered; she could feel Ivan's pain, her pain, Mike's pain. Through the intense aching, Tahlia's mind raced back to the memory of her promise to inspire others to see the joy in each moment. *How can there possibly be joy at this moment amongst all the pain and devastating loss? Will I ever feel happiness again?*

Tahlia's mind flickered, transporting her to their afternoon at the beach, playing in the water with the dolphins, Mike, and the twins laughing. Tahlia's skin tingled, and regardless of the throbbing pain emptying all life from her heart, leaving a deep gaping canyon, Tahlia could feel an underlying vibration of joy. It was as if pain and pleasure were one. Tahlia was overwhelmed; it was all too much, tears flowing into the rawness of her heart as she drifted off to sleep.

Tahlia awoke the next morning to find herself in a hospital bed, with Mike lying in a bed next to her, his head bandaged. Was he unconscious or still sleeping? Tahlia scanned the room, hoping to see the twins, praying it was all a dream. With no sign of them, Tahlia panicked, her pulse racing, the heart monitor alarm beeping.

"Jayden, Sierra, where are our twins?" she screamed hysterically.

The nurses ran in, trying to settle Tahlia.

Mike opened his eyes, alerted by Tahlia's ear-piercing screams. *Why was Tahlia hysterical?* It took Mike a moment to register that they were both lying in hospital beds, surrounded by nurses who appeared stressed out.

"Tahlia, what's wrong?" His voice was hoarse and crackly. Mike had no idea what was going on and tried to sit up but found he was too weak and sore.

Finally, Tahlia stopped screaming, her eyes glazing over, as Dr. Bradley entered.

Standing between the beds, Dr. Bradley held Tahlia's hand.

"Tahlia and Mike, you are both very fortunate, surviving the crash with only minor injuries. Mike, you have a slight head wound, about fifteen stitches, and you were unconscious for several hours."

Mike felt his head for the bandages.

"Mike, we will have to do another scan, but there are no indications of any problems at this stage. Tahlia, you escaped with a few scratches, and both of you have experienced bad bruising, which we will be monitoring over the coming days. So, some good bed rest is needed for you both."

Dr. Bradley then paused; he hated being the bearer of bad news. It was this part of his job that Dr. Bradley still found awkward and hard to do. Doing his best to deliver the information as calmly as possible, he flinched as he knew the pain these two were going to have to endure.

"I'm sorry, Mike and Tahlia; Jayden, and Sierra have both passed away."

Tahlia was motionless, she felt completely numb, even though something inside her already knew the twins were no longer with them.

Dumbfounded and confused, unsure he heard correctly, Mike said, "Doc, are you sure? What happened? Jayden and Sierra, where are they?"

"Mike, you were all in a terrible car accident. I'm so sorry there was nothing we could do. Jayden and Sierra both were deceased at the accident site. We believe they died on impact."

Mike looked at Tahlia in disbelief. Her face said it all; anguish and pain, tears pouring down her face. Mike's heart ripped open, simultaneously triggering a flood-gate of tears.

Witnessing her husband's heartbreak, Tahlia lifted her gaze, barely managing the words: "Doctor, can I get out of bed to be with my husband?"

Dr. Bradley nodded, helping Tahlia to Mike's bed. She fell into her husband's arms, both sobbing inconsolably.

Dr. Bradley ushered the nurses out of the room, "They need a little space, keep a close eye on them and give them this within the hour; it will sedate them and help them rest." He ripped a prescription off his pad.

∞ 17 ∞

AN OPEN WOUND

TAHLIA AND MIKE were in the hospital for a week. His parents did the best they could to console them both. Helena flew over to be with Tahlia and Mike. The visits were helpful, but Tahlia found herself caught in a complete daze; vacant and not hearing the conversations, everything seemed to be a blurry haze.

Why did it have to be the twins? What sort of God does this? How the hell are we ever supposed to live without Jayden and Sierra? Tahlia thought angrily. She lay there in the dark, staring at the ceiling while Mike appeared to be sleeping.

Mike heard Tahlia's sobs but did not have the strength to console her. He was dealing with the same pain and anguish. All he could do was allow his tears to flow in the darkness of the room.

"Life is so unfair; how do we ever move on from this?" uttered Tahlia between her sobs. "Please, can anyone help us?"

Tahlia let go and allowed herself to drift off, quickly finding herself being transported to Ivan's house, sitting with him in his cozy, quaint living room.

Ivan looked at her and offered a tissue. "Tahlia, my sweet, tragedy doesn't have to leave an open wound. The wounds will heal, leaving only a scar.

Tahlia was not convinced. "Ivan, how can you say that? The pain I feel right now feels like a stabbing knife twisting and gouging at my heart, ripping me apart, forming an endlessly deep canyon inside of me. You must have felt the same when you lost your wife and daughter."

"Yes, Tahlia, the wounds are raw and painful, and they take time to heal."

"This gaping wound will never heal; my children are never, ever coming back!" Tahlia yelled in anger. "I can't stand this pain! I feel so empty, so lost." Tahlia's anger burst into cascading tears.

"It's okay to feel devastated and angry Tahlia, it's natural." Ivan reached out to take Tahlia's hand to reassure her, she pulled away, the pain inside her, pushing away his kindness. Ivan smiled gently, remembering he had felt the same.

"It's not fair, why us? Jayden and Sierra were our everything. I don't know how to live without them. All I want is to cradle Jayden and Sierra in my arms, feeling the comfort of their love, but instead, I feel trapped inside a horrible consuming void. I'm scared."

"Tahlia, it's true, you are in unchartered territory and have probably never felt this depth of pain before. Your mind won't know what to do, and it will feel like there is nothing worth living for; this is part of the process."

"But Ivan, how do I possibly keep living with all this pain and loss? It will never go away." Tahlia broke into loud sobs.

"Tahlia, I understand I often asked myself the same thing when Amelie and Madeleine died. The pain was heart-wrenching, and it took a while to find space from the pain. I was clinging to my desires, wanting things to stay the way they were, one happy family, and enjoying life together. I wanted this more than anything in the entire world. The thought of imagining life without my wife and daughter felt absurd. I had expected to grow old with Amelie and Madeleine both by my side, yet this was no longer possible."

Tahlia wept, as she completely related to this.

"The more I resisted that their lives had ended, the more painful my heart ached. I felt abandoned and hollow, hating life as I spiraled downwards. My mind was having me focus on everything from a place of lack, telling me life was not worth living. The more consumed I got with these thoughts, the more painful it became; my health and life were falling apart. I didn't seem to care." Ivan caught himself reflecting, "One day, Serge, with his nuggets of wisdom, said to me, 'What happened to you, is not who you are!' I was shocked Serge would say this to me. Angrily, I fired back at him. 'Then, who am I without Amelie and Madeleine?'"

"Serge answered me quite confidently, 'You are bliss, an essence of freedom and joy! You are not this pain or what happened to you. Life comes and goes. Situations change and sometimes feelings of sadness, fear, pain, or suffering become our companions. Ivan, all these may walk alongside us, but they are not who we are, they simply are our companions for a while. Regardless of what transpires, the vibration of joy is always available to you, because you are joy.'" Ivan paused: "I remember thinking Serge was insane, as I certainly didn't feel joyful."

Tahlia's thoughts became triggered, vaguely remembering the scale of emotions Seraphina had shown her.

Ivan continued, "One day, I had to help my friend, Charlotte, give birth to her daughter. She couldn't make it to the hospital because it all happened so fast. Helping her baby daughter enter this world, I was in awe at the miracle of life. As I held this freshly new-born baby in my hands, I was filled with joy, sensing what a precious gift life is. I got a clear message, vibrating through my body: *Each soul comes here for a certain amount of time, adding value to all the lives they touch, and when they pass, that was all the time they were born to grace this earth with.* Tahlia, this message was so strong I found myself reframing death. I thought to myself, death is inevitable, and it almost always comes unexpectedly. Therefore, all we have is living in the present. Isn't that why they call it a gift?"

Tahlia's tears had stopped; she was listening intently.

"Looking at that beautiful baby, the beginning of life, I had an insight. If this baby can grow inside a mother and birth itself, and grace this earth with its presence, surely life knows what it is doing. I asked myself, what was I doing with this gift called

Life? Was I a burden on society, was I closing myself off from the magic of life because I had lost something I felt should not have happened? How could I continue to demand from life what I thought I wanted it to give me? The miracle of life knows far better than I." Ivan paused, looking at Tahlia.

"In that precious moment, I was humbled and transformed. Tahlia, I began to trust life again. I decided to do my best to live each day to the fullest, in harmony with joy. I had a choice to move through this part of my life, in pain and suffering, staying attached to my loss, or I could be grateful my life had been blessed with the presence of sweet Madeleine and my caring wife Amelie, even if it felt like only for a short time. I knew I wanted to honor the value they both had brought into my life. Amelie and Madeleine had given me so many wonderful experiences.

Eventually, I was able to feel appreciation, and that vibration of joy started to build within me; the days got better, the nights seemed more bearable. Even though my monkey-mind still played tricks on me trying to keep me locked in the pain, day-by-day, I found things in life to be grateful for. Madeleine's letter brought me comfort; the rose bush Amelie had planted bloomed; Serge, and his jovial energy showed up when I needed it. The joy didn't always last all day, but each day I saw glimmers of it and devoted myself to feeling more of it. I would notice that when I slipped into my painful thoughts, I became stronger at employing my courage, allowing the pain to bubble up and pass through me. As it drifted away, I found I would feel a sense of peace and calmness inside."

Tahlia could feel how sincere Ivan was in telling her this. She wanted to warm to his resolve to live each day to the fullest in harmony with joy, yet at the same time, Tahlia's biggest fear was demanding to be unleashed, pounding at her chest.

"Ivan, don't you feel lonely?" she sprayed out forcefully. "I'm so afraid of this loneliness, of having nothing. It feels like a massive black hole inside of me."

Ivan could sense the potency of the fear behind her words. "Tahlia, I guess there were and are still moments of loneliness, but in all honesty, I can't tell you the last time I felt the over-whelming fear of being lonely. An inner knowing, a feeling of connectedness to this gift of life has replaced the fear. Regardless of what unfolds, my mind no longer races to the fear of feeling lonely, angry or trapped. The anxiety has dissipated. Instead, I feel excited and enthusiastic, seeing every moment in life as a gift for me to unwrap and sense its beauty, a gift where I get to expand this vibration of joy in my heart and be the fullest expression of life I can be."

Ivan felt that Tahlia's energy had softened, although he noticed her mind was still struggling. Ivan placed his hand gently on her heart, "Tahlia, you can't get rid of the pain. All you can do is accept it, surrender into the loss, don't fight it. It's something you will have to pass through. Tahlia, you have the strength to move through this. Trust the void will become smaller, the wounds will heal, and they will leave a scar. However, that scar serves to remind you of the love and joy that you shared with Jayden and Sierra, reminding you of the value that they brought to yours and Mike's life. Tahlia, in time, you too will sense this joy, I know you will."

Tahlia felt something brush past, and her eyes sprang open. The sun was peeping in the hospital window, and Tahlia noticed her wooden mystery angel lying on her heart. Sitting in the chair next to her bed was Helena, her best friend.

"Morning, Tahlia. I felt you needed Seraphina today," she said, smiling at Tahlia.

Tahlia placed her hand on the angel on top of her heart and looked at Helena. "Thank you, my friend."

Tears welled up in their eyes. In unspoken words, Helena and Tahlia knew life was now on a new journey, and no matter what, their loving bond and friendship would somehow help them through.

∞ 18 ∞

RETURNING EMPTY

BACK AT HOME, wandering through the house, signs of the twins everywhere, Tahlia picked up Sierra's slipper from the middle of the lounge room floor, stroking the fake fur on it. Tahlia felt her anger rise; this wasn't supposed to happen. Their vacation should have been fun, bonding them as a family, all returning refreshed, happy, in love with life.

In a fit of anger, Tahlia threw the slipper at the wall. Mike moved toward Tahlia, embracing her, both falling into the sofa crying, releasing endless tears as reality was sinking in. Half an hour passed, and exhausted from the flow of tears, they moved into the kitchen and made a cup of coffee. Perhaps the small pleasure in life would help.

Tahlia and Mike sat motionless, staring blankly into their cups.

Summoning up the courage to break the silence, Tahlia asked, "What do we do now, Mike?"

An endless silence echoed in the room. For the first time, Mike didn't have an answer. He always had the solution, but not his time. Eventually Mike shook his head, his eyes full of heartache.

Despite her pain, Tahlia couldn't stand seeing Mike so sad. Feeling out of control and desperately wanting to fix their situation, Tahlia reached out, grabbing Mike's hand. "Mike, all I know is thank god, the universe, whomever, that you are still here with me. Together, somehow, we will find a way through this. I promise you." She leaned in, hugging him tightly, tears dripping down their faces as she stared blankly into space.

***

The following weeks and months were extremely tough. Each of them had their own way of dealing with grief.

Mike would take off by himself on motor-bike rides, tempting fate by riding as fast as he could, trying to get away from the pain. He hiked up hills, finding solitude in nature. He often would find a quiet stream he could disturb by furiously throwing rocks into it with all his might. *It's all my fault! I'm the one who had suggested to show the kids my favorite waterfall. I should have known the roads would have unsafe drivers on them.* With every rock Mike threw, he was trying to smash the water as if half blaming it, but eventually, his tears took over as he fell to his knees at the edge of the stream.

Mike's love of the beach disappeared. It no longer held any attraction for him; perhaps he was avoiding feeling his feet on the sand, afraid it would curse him with the memories of their last day together as a family. He couldn't bring himself to step foot on it. Needing an outlet for his pain, Mike became obsessed with renovating and creating things.

Tahlia tried to find the flow but just couldn't; she found herself angry at life. *What's this stupid life all about? The twins were too young to die; it's so unfair. Why us? Why our kids?* Tahlia was constantly blaming life. No matter how angry she would get, screaming, cursing, nothing changed. The fact was, her beloved twins were no longer here, Mike and herself were trying to coexist without them. Those alluring eyes with which he had once gazed at her contained only a lonely emptiness, no more exciting promise. The magic of their relationship was dying. Tahlia hated life; nothing held any interest for her; it was a considerable effort to summon up the energy to do anything.

Tahlia found herself on a never-ending roller-coaster of emotions, sometimes writing in her journal, finding it a liberating way to release her feelings. Giving free rein to her pen, allowing it to scribe out all her ugly thoughts, anger, frustration, and tears.

Other days were immobilizing; the pain was so great. Tahlia would curl up in a fetal position, feeling like an old discarded rag, scrunched up and thrown on the floor. Numb and lifeless, she would stare blankly into space for hours wishing to die.

Tahlia's doctor had given her medication, but she had thrown it in the garbage. She was never fond of medicine and thought, *What's the point in dulling my senses when they are already numb.* Tahlia needed something to lift her spirits, not dull and desensitize them.

Mike and Tahlia's' friends rallied around. Tahlia was grateful, yet at times they didn't even know what to do or say to her. She noticed that death causes people to act so differently around them. *It's like you become that woman and man who have lost your children; it becomes your identity. You stop being Tahlia and Mike.* She hated this. *Couldn't it just all go away? My heart will never heal,* Tahlia thought.

Tahlia's transporting and visions had stopped, and there were no more visitations to Ivan and Serge's wisdom. She had taken her wooden angel off her nightstand and casually thrown it on the dresser. In a way, Tahlia blamed Seraphina; she had been the one who wouldn't let her go into the light with Jayden and Sierra. Surely, Seraphina knew how much the twins meant to her.

Before throwing the mystery angel on her dresser, Tahlia had taken it to two more psychics, hoping they would give her an answer, a way out of the pain. Tahlia secretly wished they would somehow bring the twins back. All the psychics told her was that she was moving through a significant loss with a wonderful new beginning ahead. Well, if this was the wonderful new beginning, it sucked; she hated it, it wasn't what she had signed up for.

One day, in her anger, Tahlia threw herself on their bed, kicking and punching, having a full-blown tantrum, screaming at life. She kicked and pounded her fist into the bed until she could no longer, falling into a heap, arms weary and wet from inconsolable tears rolling down her face.

"What can Mike and I do to move through this? Please, please, somebody help me," she begged through broken sobs.

Subconsciously reaching her hand out trying to touch her mystery angel, Tahlia's hand dropped in exasperation, realizing it was no use; the mystery angel was not there. Tahlia's hand went limp; her eyes closed.

And then the graceful ethereal presence of Seraphina appeared. "I'm here for you, Tahlia."

Tahlia's voice was barely audible, "Please help, what can Mike and I do? We miss Jayden and Sierra; we miss the life we had. Everything has been stripped away, all the joy, our sense of purpose. We have nothing left."

"Tahlia, I know you had visions for your family, so tell me what you expected life to look like with the twins?"

"I wanted the twins to grow up happy, enjoying life, having lots of wonderful fun experiences. Mike and I wanted to grow old with them, seeing them journey through life, blossoming into their fullest potential. Being there with them through relationships and marriage, having kids of their own. I expected we would all share many birthday celebrations, the house full of their laughter, magical happy times together. Seraphina, now I have nothing! It's so unfair," Tahlia said as she broke into sobs.

Seraphina allowed Tahlia a moment to cry, releasing her unfilled expectations.

Leaning in, Seraphina took Tahlia's hand, gently caressing it. "Tahlia, I promise you; Jayden and Sierra walk beside you and Mike, their essence will always be around you."

Tahlia could feel soothing energy coming over her, a familiar feeling.

"Tahlia, life at times doesn't seem fair, because we base what it should look like on our expectations. When life unfolds differently, it's these expectations that often lead to disappointment and great pain."

Seraphina paused, mindful of delivering her words with a sense of certainty. She wanted Tahlia to understand; life always unfolds precisely as it needs to.

"Tahlia, what if I told you that Jayden and Sierra's souls were needed elsewhere? Their souls had other plans that would allow them to expand and grow into their fullest potential. The twins needed to leave so you and Mike can blossom into your fullest potential, too. Life knows you and Mike have an enormous amount of love and strength to come through this, and the twins knew this, too. Tahlia, trust life, trust creation. Together you and Mike will start a new life full of adventure, and through those adventures, you will bring joy to many people. You will enrich and inspire more lives than you can ever imagine."

Tahlia heard Seraphina but wasn't convinced. "We were happy bringing Jayden and Sierra joy. How will this loss help us bring joy to others?"

"Beautiful Tahlia, the how is not up to me or you, it is up to life itself, which is always changing and unfolding. One universal truth, I know for sure, is that life never gives us something we don't have the strength to come through. The choice is ours, whether we kick and scream, dragging ourselves, resisting and clinging, or we can gracefully move through the constant unfolding, experiencing, and participating with joy."

Tahlia had a momentary flashback to Ivan. Hadn't he said something similar? Hadn't he decided to embrace life with joy?

"Tahlia, take a deep breath. What would you like to feel right now?"

Tahlia thought for a moment. "Peace, something to be happy about."

Seraphina flashed her hand in front of Tahlia's face; instantly, she felt a soothing sense of peace, which morphed into a warm fuzzy feeling of joy. Tahlia was surprised by this feeling – joy, something her heart had not felt for months. The elated happiness she felt was similar to when they were all swimming among the dolphins in Hawaii. Suddenly Tahlia's brain took her back to the memory of seeing Jayden and Sierra lying dead in the car; her joy vanished. Tears began to flow down her cheeks.

"Tahlia, can you see how the peace and joy already exist, yet when you went back and focused on the past, the sadness took over again?"

Breathing deeply, Tahlia sensed clarity in Seraphina's words. "So, my memories are keeping me locked in all the sadness?"

"Yes, Tahlia, your memories and expectations of how you thought life should be."

Seraphina placed her hand on Tahlia's forehead, "Do you remember the emotional scale we visited where sadness and joy existed alongside each other?"

Tahlia nodded, vaguely recalling.

"Thoughts and memories can trigger your sadness, so can expectations you perceived were unfulfilled. Allowing these to bubble up and pass through you without being attached or giving them meaning is the way to move up the emotional vibration scale, thus allowing you to feel joy."

Seraphina became silent as she saw Tahlia reflecting.

"Tahlia, you asked what's the one thing you and Mike can do to move through this. Tahlia, be present, surrendering, and releasing your likes and dislikes of how you think life should be, allow the universe to expand its infinite possibilities to you. The key is to keep asking yourself, 'What can I do to be the greatest expression of joy in this moment?' By focusing on this question, you will experience the freedom and joy you seek, navigating your way through the darkest moments in ways you would have never imagined."

Seraphina placed her hand on Tahlia's heart, allowing this to land and seeing her words vibrate into Tahlia's body.

Tahlia felt a calm sense of peace and acceptance, an inner knowingness of what to do to move forward through her loss. It was going to take some practice, but there is a way forward. Ivan had shown her this.

"Tahlia, Tahlia!" Mike's voice held some kind of excitement a sense of urgency. His energy pulled her out of her vision, Tahlia jumped out of bed, racing out to see Mike standing in the lounge room. He was holding something unusual in his hands.

"Tahlia, look what I've created, out of Jayden and Sierra's favorite toys." Mike's voice held an air of enthusiasm, "Jayden's fast boat and Sierra's angel fairy – the same ones they had been playing with the night before the vacation."

Tahlia gasped, she didn't even know he was doing this, he had kept it a secret from her.

"What do you think?" Proudly, he handed the ornament to Tahlia.

She marveled at how skilled Mike had been, melding both together. He had mounted the boat on what appeared to be an ocean of waves beautifully carved out of wood, painted turquoise blue. The back half of the boat was intact, surrounded by the water. From the mid-deck toward the bow, Sierra's fairy angel rose out of it. With his skilled hands and creativity, Mike had beautifully morphed these two together. Tahlia could feel the love and attention he had poured into this masterpiece. She was speechless.

"Honey, do you like it?"

Tahlia nodded, a gentle tear of joy falling out of the corner of her eye. Mike took his finger and traced across it, wiping the tear from her face, tenderly leaning in to kiss Tahlia's cheek.

Finding her voice, Tahlia allowed her appreciation to flow, "Mike, I love it. You are a true craftsman, talented in so many ways."

"I had help, the twins guided me along the way," Mike replied, trying to deflect tears that were welling in his eyes.

"It's beautiful. The twins would love it. I love you."

Both started to cry, but the energy of their tears felt different this time. They were tears of joy. Tahlia and Mike hugged and kissed; it was as if something had broken free; they both felt the release. Squeezing each other tightly, they lingered in the embrace, cherishing this new freedom, feeling the love of Jayden and Sierra with them.

"Let's find the perfect place for it," Tahlia said, taking the ornament, trying out a few spaces, finally placing it in the center of the sideboard, next to a picture of the twins.

Mike smiled in approval.

"Tahlia, I was hoping we could name it. All boats should have a name." Mike continued with enthusiasm, "Tahlia, the entire time I carved and worked on the ornament, the name Joyful Adventures kept ringing in my ears. What do you think?"

Tahlia smiled from ear to ear. "Joyful Adventures is perfect."

Mike raised his arms in excitement, pulling out of his pocket a small piece of silver metal. Engraved on it was a symbol of a star, Joyful Adventures, and another star. Mike pulled out a small tube of glue, lining the metal before he positioned the small plaque onto the hull of the boat. It felt complete.

Tahlia and Mike stood back, looking at his creation, both feeling a deep sense of connection and love for Jayden and Sierra.

At dinner that night, the energy between them was lighter; they were laughing and smiling; something had shifted for them both. Tahlia would never know precisely what magic her ethereal friend Seraphina had bestowed upon them, but she knew it was exactly what they needed.

∞ 19 ∞
A SHIFT IN ENERGY

TAHLIA AND MIKE found themselves participating in life more, instead of just existing and feeling trapped in reactions to grief and loss. Joyful Adventures, the ornament, was a reminder for Mike and Tahlia to choose joy. Each time one of them would pass the ornament, it bought a smile to their face as if Jayden and Sierra were sprinkling them with love.

Yes, Tahlia's heart still ached, at times crumbling in pain. As often as she could, Tahlia would allow the pain to pass through her, not being attached to its stories, surrendering and bringing herself to a place of acceptance, consciously choosing to feel joy at least once every day. Was it easy? No, was it worth it? Yes.

Usually, waves of memories, stress, or angry outbursts triggered her tears, which she tried her best to move through or transform. In the very dark moments, joy seemed so elusive, not a spark to be found anywhere. Tahlia had to focus on surrendering; it was a conscious effort. Daily meditation became part of Tahlia's routine; day by day, she practiced visualizing, instructing her imagination to create a new happy, adventurous life for her and Mike. Tahlia allowed her imagination to take them to a place that felt joyful and fun.

Tahlia had come to notice that everyone around her had their own opinion of what she should do to grieve. Her work colleagues and other acquaintances thought she was in denial, not comprehending how Tahlia could focus on joy. But Tahlia knew this was not their journey to deal with. Tahlia was finding the process a very individual one, with Mike processing things in his unique way. Mike had thrown his energy into renovating, venting his anger and grief by knocking down walls and recreating.

One of the most challenging conversations came when they were looking at the twins' room, deciding what to do.

"Tahlia, are you ready to change this room?" Mike softly approached the sensitive subject.

Tahlia knew the conversation was coming, but now that it was here, she didn't know how she felt. Her head sent her into all sorts of thoughts. A big loud NO pounded in her head. *No, the bedroom is Jayden and Sierra's room; we need to leave it as it is. If we change it, that means it's final; they are never coming back. Of course, they're not coming back, stupid, they're dead.* Tahlia couldn't believe how cruel her thoughts were, embarrassed and hoping she hadn't said them aloud, she lowered her head into her hands, crying.

Mike watched, not knowing what to say, he decided to honor the silence and let Tahlia cry. In his heart, he knew they had to start making a change.

Tahlia eventually raised her head and took a breath, "I don't know Mike; it just seems so final." Tahlia looked at Mike to see what he was feeling.

Mike surprised Tahlia by saying, "I know this isn't easy, Tahlia, but no time will ever be the right time." His resolve was firm, yet Mike delivered it lovingly. "Tahlia, we can't keep looking at this as the twins' bedroom, being reminded every time we walk by. We have to start to move on. Yes, Jayden and Sierra were our life, but now...." His voice trailed off as he picked up a picture of the twins playing at the beach. "We need to create a home that feels happy to be in, not morbid."

Tahlia raised her head and allowed her eyes to look around the room. She hated the morbid feeling hovering over their house like a big dark cloud, Tahlia longed for their house to feel fresh and inviting again. It was obvious why most of their friends had stopped visiting, the house was depressing. Tahlia yearned for a home where their friends felt comfortable visiting, a place where they all could enjoy themselves again. Mike was right; Tahlia knew for both their mental and emotional health they needed to find a way to move on.

Cleaning out the twins' room was challenging for both Mike and Tahlia. Even though Mike had encouraged the decision, it wasn't easy for him to let go of the twins' belongings. Mike would keep piling up different items to keep. Tahlia saw a lot of the things as stuff that only enforced painful memories.

"I have an idea, Mike, instead of keeping all these items, let's take photos of the twins' things we cherish, and I can turn the pictures into a book, something we will have forever."

Mike agreed. He was thankful Tahlia had shared her inspiration, it made parting with some of Jayden and Sierra's belongings easier for him.

Tahlia decided to make a fun game of it, taking pictures in different quirky angles. She placed Jayden's favorite beanie on Mike's head and made him pull a face. Mike took a photo of Sierra's ballet shoes on Pookey, her big stuffed bear, while Tahlia tried to make it dance. Tahlia's favorite photo was Sierra's princess doll in the horse carriage, with Jayden's stuffed dog chasing them. Mike and Tahlia found themselves laughing and coming up with unique ways to part with those cherished items.

Throughout the process of taking the photos and letting go of the twins' things, Tahlia felt like Jayden and Sierra were still alive, reminding her and Mike of the beautiful connection they all share. Realizing there were so many happy moments, Tahlia thought, *this is going to be a big book*!

Tahlia would get lost in all their sweet memories as she pieced together the photo album on her computer. Creating both a hardcover book and a digital copy, that she set to revolve on her computer screen continuously, Tahlia was inspired to name the book *Joyful Moments*. Mike and Tahlia both loved the book, finding comfort in it, especially on days when emotions got the better of them.

With all the renovations and changes, it felt as if they were finally discarding that dark depressive cloud, moving into a brighter future.

Before long, they were painting the twins' old room, which Mike, with his skilled craftsmanship, had transformed beautifully into a new guest room. Mike had built a long wooden bench seat under the window that could serve as a day bed overlooking the back garden. Together Mike and Tahlia decorated it with warm furnishings, creating an enticing new space. Mike, with help from his friends, extended the entertainment room, giving the house a lovely indoor-outdoor feel. Eventually, Tahlia and Mike began inviting friends to visit again, adding new joy to their home.

During this transition, Tahlia had thrown herself into work. She felt like work was the one constant that grounded her through the loss and massive changes. Losing herself in scripts and enhancing the stories seemed to give Tahlia a break away from her pain, until now. But of late Tahlia had discovered nothing was flowing, it was like her imagination was on hold, words were struggling to formulate, she couldn't get through her workload, scripts continually being returned to be reworded. Tahlia overheard whispers in the office, "Do you think she is coping? Perhaps she really shouldn't be here."

Joyous Adventures, the ornament, plus the creation of the book *Joyful Moments*, along with the house improvements, had all been good distractions. Mike seemed to have been able to process his sadness through his handy work by taking his aggression out on the renovations, turning the house into something new. For some strange reason, Tahlia's creativity seemed blocked. No matter how hard she tried to tap into her imagination, it appeared elusive; she felt as if she were an imposter.

A part of Tahlia was afraid to sit still and get close to her wounds of the twins' death, afraid it would break her completely apart. Tahlia, never one to succumb to a victim consciousness, felt that by going there, she would end up playing that role. Tahlia's work had helped her push away the wound and any possibility of becoming a victim; surely by now, it was healing.

Not today. Something in the whispers, the false smiles from people, the pressure of everyone else's deadlines, being locked out of her imagination – all seemed to grate on her. She felt a storm brewing inside.

Caleb came over with another returned script. "Sorry, Tahlia, the producers feel this needs more creative drama, and they want it back by tonight before their meeting."

Without warning, Tahlia stood up, slamming her hands on the desk, yelling, "I've had enough of all these demands!" Pushing her chair back, she stormed out, rushing to the restroom.

Office staff scurried out of the way of her anger, turning as Tahlia stormed past, baffled at what had happened.

Helena came running after her. "Tahlia, what's happened?"

Tahlia broke down in tears. "Helena, I can't do this anymore: other people's deadlines, the whispers, the pressure, trying to be someone I'm not, pretending I have it all together."

Helena handed her tissues as Tahlia wiped her eyes. "I thought I was moving on, but I feel trapped in this vortex of coping, aimlessly treading water. I can't get out of it." Blowing her nose, trying to clear her tears, she went on. "Helena, I need to feel like me again. I don't know what to do."

Helena had had a feeling this moment would come one day, so thinking quickly on her feet, she said, "Tahlia, let's head out for some fresh air. Stay here, fix yourself up, I'll grab our bags." Helena raced off.

Adjusting her hair, Tahlia caught a glimpse of her eyes in the mirror; they appeared hollow and dull. Where was that spark of enthusiasm? How she so wanted it to return.

Helena led Tahlia to the park, where they sat on the soft grass under a big tree. Helena had brought water and a bag of chocolate-coated blueberries; she was listening to Tahlia.

"Helena, I've been doing the best I can, trying to cope, but it's so hard. I can't do this anymore." Tahlia took a deep breath, doing her best not to become a blubbering mess again. "My life is dull and mundane. I can't believe the birth and loss of Jayden and Sierra was all meant to lead Mike and me here, to this empty, boring space. Mike and I used to be so adventurous. I miss those days. I want my spark for life back."

Helena could feel that Tahlia was in pain and hated seeing her best friend feeling so devastated and lost.

Tahlia continued, spilling out her thoughts. "I feel like I need something different, I don't want it always to be Tahlia and Mike the couple who lost their twins. This label; I'm fed up with it, there has to be more to life." Tahlia paused, looking up at Helena, "It's a festering wound I can't control or fix." A fresh barrage of tears released from Tahlia's eyes.

Helena put her hand under Tahlia's chin and lifted it to the sky, looking into her eyes. "Tahlia, you don't have to fix it, but you can help it heal, you can surrender to it and eventually create something new."

Tahlia pulled her chin from Helena's hand, snapping at her best friend, "How the hell am I supposed to do that? I've tried everything!"

Tahlia was embarrassed for snapping at Helena, bursting into sobs she fell face-down on the earth, pounding the ground with her fists, letting it all pour out of her heart.

Helena rested a reassuring hand on the back of Tahlia's heart, simply being present, allowing her friend to release it. Helena began humming sweetly and softly, as a peaceful state came over Tahlia. It was a familiar, serene, calm, graceful feeling.

Tahlia saw a picture in her mind, flashing back to when she was a child, riding a white horse on the carousel. Tahlia's Nan and Pop waved at her each time she went around. How she loved them, they were always there encouraging her. Instantly Nan and Pop morphed into Ivan and Serge. Tahlia blinked, and behind Ivan and Serge, she saw Seraphina. Tahlia was embarrassed; had they been listening to her, pouring out all her pain, snapping at Helena?

The carousel slowed, stopping directly in front of Ivan and Serge. Seraphina walked over, gently placing her hand on Tahlia's shoulder. Seraphina's touch vibrated through Tahlia's entire body, giving her goosebumps.

"Tahlia, it's okay, there are things in life we can't control. Every single person will experience loss of some form throughout their life. As harsh as life might feel at times, each and everyone's pain is relevant to what they are going through. No one's loss or suffering is greater than another's; it's a journey," explained Seraphina.

Serge piped up, offering his wisdom, "Tahlia, your past doesn't have to define your future. You have the choice not to let what happened to you become your identity; it isn't you. Instead, see it as something that you had the experience to become more of who you truly are. Tahlia, you are the one who creates your future."

Ivan added, "Sooner or later, you get to the point where you've had enough of all the suffering and struggle. Tahlia, it's at this moment you have the choice to surrender, accepting this situation is what it is. Know that no amount of struggle, resistance, or force will change it. As you surrender into accepting, you make space to set a new intention."

Tahlia saw herself hovering above her body lying on the ground under the tree, surrendering into her fears, pain, and frustrations. As she allowed them just to be, Tahlia let go, sensing mother earth embracing them all. A wave of complete acceptance came over her, and at that moment, she saw Jayden and Sierra happily playing, enjoying wherever they were. It was a pretty place, very colorful, surrounded by nature.

She heard Jayden say to Sierra, "This place is so cool and fun, I hope mum and dad are happy."

Sierra replied, giggling, "Of course they are happy, Jayden, all they want is for us to be happy."

Tahlia's heart melted, and instead of tears and pain, she felt the love for her children filling every cell of her body. Embracing the moment, Tahlia marveled at their sweet, innocent, delightful souls. She was thankful for all the joyful memories of them, their smiling faces, funny little habits, their curious ways. Jayden and Sierra had taught her and Mike so much. Tahlia felt extremely grateful she and Mike had experienced the chance to love the twins and be loved by them.

In front of Tahlia appeared a golden path. Tahlia looked around, reaching out for the twins, and for a split second, she panicked. Jayden and Sierra were gone.

Ivan, Serge, and Seraphina were witnessing Tahlia's experience.

Encouraging her forward, Ivan whispered, "Tahlia, I was able to rise through the pain and take a new path. I know you can too."

Tahlia looked around, glancing once again at the golden path. In the pit of her stomach, Tahlia could feel fear of the unknown rising, the uncertainty of what lay ahead without the twins. Yet strangely, Tahlia's heart was at peace, this golden path graciously beckoning her forward.

Seraphina spoke, soothing her, "Tahlia, this fear and pain is your ego resisting moving forward. Your heart knows it wants to be happy."

Tahlia nodded. *Yes, she wanted more than anything to be happy; she wanted to enjoy life again.*

"Tahlia, love, joy, and gratitude will change your vibration, sending out energy in alignment with what you seek; freedom and happiness. These vibrations are like signals, magnetizing many new opportunities. Tahlia, acknowledge your fear, knowing it is a way of reminding you to let go and embrace joy. Focus your attention on being the greatest expression of joy you can be, following your curiosity, as you take one step at a time." Seraphina stood on the edge of the golden path, holding out her hand.

Tahlia knew she had a choice. She could stay in the lonely dark space of the past, or take Seraphina's hand and continue to walk forward, with life's unfolding journey. Tahlia recalled those alluring eyes she had once followed, shining a sense of inner beauty, beckoning her to follow them again. Hesitantly, Tahlia stepped onto the golden path. Taking her first step, Tahlia felt an undeniable inner beauty filling her with a hint of joy and excitement.

"Tahlia, the sun is setting, are you ready to go?" Helena gently coaxed Tahlia to return.

Pulling her focus back, Tahlia sat up, with calm relief on her face. "Yes, I'm ready. Helena, thank you so much for being there for me. I'm sorry I snapped at you." Tahlia leaned in and hugged Helena. "You somehow always know what I need."

Helena smiled. "Speaking of that, check out the carousel. Do you want a ride?"

Tahlia was shocked by the synchronicity; did Helena know about her vision? Grabbing Tahlia's hand, Helena paid their money, and together they jumped on the carousel. Two women, feeling like excited young girls, laughing as the carousel spun in circles. Tahlia was riding the same white horse.

That evening Tahlia cleared space on her bedside table, gently placing the wooden mystery angel on it. Tahlia looked at it fondly, smiling as she allowed her fingers to trace the angel's delicately carved hands in prayer. Slipping into bed exhausted yet happy, Tahlia felt Mike wrap his arms tenderly around her, snuggling in. He, too, could feel Tahlia had finally broken through, sensing she had a new inner glow.

Tahlia's last thoughts before she drifted off were, *I'm ready to create a life I love.*

∞ 20 ∞

EMBRACE CHANGE

IT WAS THE weekend; Tahlia had awoken with a new vigor for life and a seed of curiosity planted in her mind. What did women do with the next part of life after their kids were grown up and left home? How did these women continue with life?

Recognizing a similarity between them and her situation, Tahlia was curious. Tahlia knew from her body clock that it was too late for her and Mike to have more children, and they had decided that neither of them wanted anymore. Yet part of Tahlia felt a bit lost without her identity of being a mother; her life felt meaningless.

Tahlia found herself Googling empty nesters, curious to see how others moved on in life and found a new purpose. Swamped with Facebook groups and loads of information, Tahlia didn't resonate with any of it and was getting disheartened. She heard a voice inside her saying, "Tahlia, life contains many different chapters; there is always a way to find the magic." She could sense Seraphina coming through, guiding her to keep searching. Tahlia scrolled through the internet, stumbling over a blog title popping out like a neon sign.

Wanting a new chapter in life: have the kids left home, and you're not sure what's next?

Tahlia clicked on the blog and began to read:

"For most of us these days, life has taken on a new era. It's time we started focusing on creating a new chapter, a new purpose for ourselves once our children leave home.

"Over time, our life span has become longer and longer due to better living standards, improved health care, sanitation, accessibility to clean running water, and nutritious foods.

"In the 1800s, life expectancy wavered between 30 and 40 years of age. During the 1900s, we saw this increase to 50-60 years, and now in today's society, our average life span is between 78-88 years.

"Originally, our mindset and conditioning of society was to grow up, get a job, a house, have a family, enjoy them while you are young, and then basically get ready to die. Death seemed upon us relatively soon once the children left home, if they left home."

Tahlia had a little laugh; *the author is rather blunt and straight to the point*, she thought, continuing to read on.

"Centuries ago becoming an empty nester never really happened because we died at an early age before we experienced all the children leaving home. Also, living in tribes and communities, we seemed to have a purpose, weaving our skills together in the fabric of our environment.

"Life in the 21st century is different now, we are living much longer, especially when you look at the above statistics. In modern-day life, most of our children have left home by our mid 40's. Therefore, we have another good 40 years to live, especially since the average woman is living to 86 years of age.

"Let's stop and think about this for a minute...

"You grow up, get a job, (now you're in your 20's) fall in love, have some children (now you're in your 30's) juggle your kids, husband, and career, Launching into your 40's, you feel this is your heyday. As you arrive in the mid to late 40's, suddenly those children to whom you have devoted most of your time, leave and get their own life. Of course, they still need you at times, but you no longer have to be their taxi/Uber driver, chef, housemaid, washing, and ironing. Instantly time frees up for you, there seems to be some form of relief from all that juggling, yet you begin to feel empty, still clutching at your identity of super mum.

"Society never showed us what to do next, how to fill that void. In most cases, people's focus becomes more about surviving until they die. No one ever showed us that now in our '50s we can begin a new chapter of living, trying new things, having a new purpose.

"Ladies, I'm here to help you see we have years of living to do. I would love to shine light upon a new perspective, a new way to approach this:

~ Imagine ~

"The children have left home; your sense of purpose has vanished. However, you find yourself with all this freedom, realizing that you still have possibly another 40 years of living to do. You are in the kitchen, surrounded by loads of your favorite ingredients with no recipe, no demands. You get to decide what to make, not the kids, not the hubby, not the cat or dog, not even your boss or career. It's like you now have the opportunity to start to play, to examine your life, the ingredients you love, going deep into your heart, reconnecting with your dreams. You're excited to start creating something new. What do you want to create? What does it taste, smell, feel like? Allow yourself to imagine.

"At first, this may seem foreign, as your life revolved around others, putting their needs before yours. Can you embrace this wonderful opportunity to create a brand-new chapter of life, a delicious new dish? Something you get to put your stamp on, a new you, a new way of being. If the truth is known, you have probably yearned for this at some stage in the last decade. I invite you to begin dreaming again."

Tahlia took a deep breath; she so resonated with this women's words.

"Some of you may become grandparents and happily choose to revolve your lives around the grandkids, filling that void. For others, you have this new freedom, an uncharted territory that may feel a little uncertain. One thing I know to be true, having lived through life's twists and turns, you have an inner sense of knowing yourself intimately. You have been able to navigate life's ups and downs, becoming resourceful, growing through those challenges. The unfolding of life hasn't broken you; upon reflection, your challenges may have seemed incredibly hard, but you are stronger for having been through them."

Tahlia paused, contemplating how true. As painful as it was, the tragedy of the twins dying and Tahlia believing her heart would never heal, didn't break them. Tahlia and Mike had become stronger; the bond between them had strengthened, creating a more significant bridge of trust. The love they shared felt more profound, more reliable, more enjoyable. Even though Tahlia and Mike had survived their worst nightmare, they had found moments of happiness. Life seemed to be still unfolding in a way she had never imagined.

Tahlia continued to read:

"...Ladies (and men), it is time for us to embrace a new chapter of history in life. Where we truly get to be all that we are, where we have the freedom and wisdom to be able to bring our unique gifts into the world and do what we have always wanted. I believe we are now living in extraordinary times where we get to write more scenes and chapters to our life; we get to direct them, not the conditioning of society.

"Personally, I've seen a lot of women feeling lost and invisible in their later years; they have forgotten what lights them up. You may be one of them, letting the happenings of life lay like dust over your precious gifts. If you were to vacuum that dust off, what would you find? What will your next chapter of life look like?

Action steps:

- Take time during the week to entertain your dreams

- Journal out your thoughts

- Take a walk in nature

- Stay alert for the inspiration as it comes your way

"My friends, please don't leave your gifts on the shelf covered in dust, the world is waiting for them.

"Until next week…create a magical day xo M"

Tahlia was fascinated, resonating strongly with M's insights. She's right; there are many more chapters of life to live, perhaps it was time for a new chapter in her and Mike's life. Tahlia felt the words vibrating through her body.

**

Passing her hand over the ornament Joyful Adventures, Tahlia reflected on the whirlwind of her life; finding her mystery angel, meeting Mike, marrying, giving birth to the twins. Watching and nurturing Jayden and Sierra as they grew into their unique personalities, sending them to school and then their passing. Now, two years since their passing, where had all those years gone? Tahlia contemplated her mystery angel; this gift, why was she given it? Did the angel have anything to do with all this? Since the arrival of her wooden angel, Tahlia had experienced visits from Seraphina, Ivan, and Serge. All of which helped bring her a sense of hope and clarity throughout all these challenges. *How intriguing,* she thought; *just when we think we have settled into a place of comfort, along comes change, sometimes by choice and sometimes not, life just doing life. I guess the only guarantee in life is change*, thought Tahlia.

Taking a seat on the comfortable armchair, Tahlia allowed the rays of the sun filtering in through the window to dance on her skin. She could feel the winds of change were upon her.

Pondering how change often feels scary, the fear of the unknown, no certainty, then at other times change felt exciting and stimulating. In truth, Tahlia's curiosity loved change. *So, if change is the only guarantee in life, what can I do to flow with it more? How can I be more willing to embrace change from a joyful, excited, curious place, rather than fighting change, full of fear? I wonder, what's the best approach to navigate change?* Tahlia closed her eyes, the warm sun comforting her as she allowed herself to drift off….

Tahlia found herself on a golden path, her hand on a round brass doorknob, not sure whether to open it.

Seraphina appeared beside her. "Hello, Tahlia, are you going to go in?"

"I don't know," Tahlia stalled for words. "I've been wondering should I walk through the doorway of change or wait for it to open. I can feel it coming, and I want to be able to embrace change with ease this time, but I'm scared."

Tahlia looked at Seraphina, "I'm scared it won't be what I want, that I won't be able to control it."

Tahlia felt a brief stab to her heart, remembering the change that was thrust upon her when the twins passed.

Seraphina took Tahlia's hands in hers. "Tell me, Tahlia, what dreams do you have for you and Mike."

Tahlia looked down at her feet then up towards the sky, gathering her strength. "Seraphina, I would love for Mike and me to be happy. To have fun adventures, exploring nature, traveling the world. I want us to laugh again, finding the magic wherever we go. To contribute happiness to the planet in some way."

Seraphina looked on lovingly as Tahlia continued: "I want us to feel joy, peace, and freedom again. But Seraphina, I don't know how to create that. I'm worried if we make a change, life will throw us another huge challenge." Tahlia sighed deeply.

Seraphina smiled, "Tahlia, I agree adversity can be challenging, but it is what makes us stronger, helping us to grow."

Re-adjusting her posture, Seraphina looked Tahlia directly in the eyes, "Tahlia, regardless of whatever change occurs, you can be assured there is always an element of peace and freedom within change; it is guaranteed."

Tahlia was not convinced, "What do you mean, Seraphina? How do we embrace change, or feel peace when there is so much uncertainty? Particularly amidst the chaos, or when the change is not what we want. What happens if life turns out bad again?"

"Tahlia, it's the thoughts of wanting things to be or feel a certain way that cause you pain, fear, and anxiety. When your thoughts are resisting, what is happening?"

Seraphina could see Tahlia was trying to grasp what she was saying.

"Tahlia, being open to accepting is key, allowing the experience to be, without deciding whether you like or dislike it. Everything has its beauty, even the things we don't like." Seraphina allowed the silence between them to build.

Tahlia wanted to understand this; she was doing her best to find clarity in Seraphina's words.

"Is there a simple way to accept it?" asked Tahlia.

"Your breath. Tahlia, start by following your breath, be aware of taking deep inhales and long exhales. Your breath helps you to surrender and allows your thoughts to be present in the moment. Being present in the moment drops your resistance, creating freedom and space, in turn allowing you to accept what is unfolding, regardless of your likes or dislikes. It is in this space where you feel the peace, creating room for inspiration."

Is it really that simple? thought Tahlia, as she took some deep inhales and exhales.

"Tahlia, the peace comes from being able to be open to change and looking at it with a sense of awe and wonderment. Remember when you found yourself pregnant with the twins? The miracle of life happened; new life was created."

Tahlia touched her stomach, realizing that the birth of the twins was out of her control. Truth be known, she would have chosen only to have single births rather than twins. Yet life with twins unfolded regardless of her preference. During her pregnancy, she had come to a stage of accepting; this is what it is. Tahlia recalled from that moment on she was able to appreciate the miracle of two lives growing inside her with awe and wonder. She had embraced the twins and became excited.

Seraphina interrupted Tahlia's thoughts. "Tahlia, change always brings an element of uncertainty; your role is to accept the unknown, to embrace it with joy, trusting and flowing peacefully along the journey."

Where is my diary? thought Tahlia, feeling the need to capture this wisdom.

Seraphina's presence began to fade into the distance.

Tahlia opened her eyes and glanced toward the table next to her. Sitting on the table was her diary and favorite pen. She smiled to herself. Picking up her pen, Tahlia began writing in her journal:

"...*View change as a constant unfolding journey, always creating something new. Embrace change by accepting this is what it is, breathing in the moment. Know that peace exists within change always! Breathe until you sense that peace, creating space for inspiration. It's my choice to embrace change joyfully."* ♥

∞ 21 ∞

NAVIGATE LIFE'S FLOW

TAHLIA'S NEW INSIGHT enhanced her enthusiasm and creativity, renewing her zest for life. Mike noticed Tahlia's glow immediately, reminding him of when they first met. Reflecting on all the fun, magical adventures they had shared, Mike couldn't help but smile. He was thrilled; Tahlia had turned a corner.

Mike had worked through blaming himself for Jayden and Sierra's death; after all, he was driving and had suggested they see the waterfalls in the rain. For several months the guilt consumed him; it wouldn't leave. Once the accident report came back, showing it was a hundred percent the truck driver's negligence, Mike slowly was able to let go of his guilt. They decided to settle out of court because neither Mike nor Tahlia wanted to relive any of the ugly details. Regardless of how much Mike and Tahlia were hurting, their compassionate hearts knew the truck driver was also suffering.

However, it had taken Mike a while longer to forgive the truck driver. Every wall Mike smashed down in the renovations of their house seemed to release him from the anger he had toward the driver. Mike was thankful for the chance to vent and the ability to funnel his energy into creating something new from these feelings.

Throughout it all, Mike had been concerned about Tahlia; he knew she was pretending to cope. But now, Tahlia's new turn-around gave Mike hope. The change in her energy brought a smile to Mike's heart, making Tahlia more attractive. Mike found himself wanting to make more time to be with her. It was as if their friendship and love had grown to another level. With these renewed feelings toward his wife, Mike decided now would be a good time to bring up the subject that had been on his mind for a few months.

"Tahlia, let's go; I've got a surprise for you," called Mike, waiting at the doorway with a backpack in hand. "I'll meet you on the motorbike."

"Where are we going?" she called, chasing after him.

"Somewhere fun." Mike handed Tahlia her helmet, and together they jumped on Mike's road bike.

Tahlia loved being on the back of the bike; it had been ages since they had been on a ride together. Riding around, Tahlia immersed herself in the scenes, a beautiful sunny day with an expansive blue sky, loads of people out and about making the most of the brilliant weather. Tahlia loved the wind on her face and the freedom she felt.

Mike found the perfect spot, a little grassy hill overlooking the Marina. He pulled a blanket out of his backpack, setting up a little picnic he had thrown together. Tahlia was impressed as Mike poured them each a glass of cider. She sat on the blanket, leaning into him, enjoying the sun, savoring the moment and the view.

"Tahlia, what do you feel about packing up our house and sailing around the Mediterranean?"

Tahlia was caught by surprise, nearly spilling her cider. "That's a huge life change. Do you mean in a couple of years or now?"

Mike was smiling, nodding his head.

Tahlia knew her hubby's sense of adventure, how much he loved boats and the ocean. Sailing came as no surprise; it was the thought of leaving, being in Europe, far away from her friends. Surely, Mike didn't mean now. They had only recently finished the renovations; she was finally enjoying their home again, and it felt like they both were adjusting to life without Jayden and Sierra.

Mike could see Tahlia's mind at work. "Tahlia, why are we staying here? I mean, life has become a little more bearable, yet it still feels like we are just surviving in a place where there will always be a big massive void. I'm not sure I want us to continue in this grind, do you?" Mike looked Tahlia directly in the eyes, "I would love us to have a new adventure, a fresh start."

Tahlia could see he had thought long and hard about this, and she could sense his longing. Tahlia thought, *Mike has a point; whenever we are in the house, it will always hold strong memories of the twins.*

Mike broke Tahlia's depth of thought, "Tahlia, I truly think it is time to move on. We both need a change."

How appropriate, Tahlia thought, remembering her visit with Seraphina. She had known she felt the winds of change; she just didn't quite expect this.

"Mike, it's obvious you have been putting a lot of thought into this, tell me more about the adventure you envisage for us," she asked gently.

"I pictured us selling our home, buying a boat we love and sailing it around the south of Europe. Trading this routine life, for one with spontaneity and excitement," Mike smiled enthusiastically. "Imagine all the adventures we can have! Different cultures and places that we get to explore, the sense of freedom. Tahlia, it will be a way for us to be in love with life again."

Tahlia was contemplating the vision Mike painted, as she peered toward the Marina.

"What type of boat? What would it look like?"

"I love catamarans and know you will too, they have more space and are like an apartment on the water. Look, just like that one heading out." Mike cradled her in his arms, pointing toward the sailing boat, bobbing on the water.

Tahlia could feel how much Mike wanted to do this. She felt herself resisting the change. However, she didn't want to dampen his spirits. "Mike, it sounds like a lovely adventure, can I have a little time to think about it?"

Mike was crushed as he was sure Tahlia would want this; he thought she was ready. The old Tahlia would have jumped at the chance.

Tahlia noticed how rejected Mike seemed; she wanted to kick herself for allowing her fear and hesitation to dampen his dream. Tahlia took a deep breath,

"Mike, perhaps when we get home, you can show me some pictures of the boats you are thinking about."

Mike's face lit up; he knew there was a glimmer of hope that Tahlia may jump on board with his dream. Giving her a big kiss, he whispered into her ear, "I can't wait to start a new life with you again, Tahlia."

Together they melted into each other's arms.

On the motorbike ride home, Tahlia found her thoughts erratically bouncing around, from being excited to explore Europe, to the daunting task of learning how to sail, not to mention all the things she needed to coordinate, organize, and do before they even got on the boat. All this and she hadn't even agreed yet.

Arriving home, Tahlia immediately rang Helena, as she felt the need to confide in her best friend. "Can I come over?"

"Of course, I'll make us a cocktail." Helena could sense her friend needed to chat.

Helena had set up the sun lounges and mojitos by the pool. They had barely gotten comfortable when Tahlia started.

"Helena, can you believe Mike wants us to sell the house and buy a boat to live on in the Mediterranean?" Tahlia was in a spin.

"And what is wrong with that?" Helena asked, sipping her mojito, trying to contain a smile.

"We just finished the renovations; our careers are here; it's not the right time, not yet." Tahlia's fear was feeding all her excuses to Helena.

"Maybe it is the perfect timing, Tahlia. With the renovations finished, the house is very presentable and ready to sell. You haven't been happy at work for a while. Tahlia, you know you need a change." Helena was calling Tahlia's bluff.

It worked. Tahlia looked at Helena, voicing a big sigh. "Maybe Mike is right; he looked so excited when he was painting me the vision. I know he truly wants to do this."

"And he wants to do it with you, Tahlia, his wife, the one he loves beside him. This could be exactly what you both need." It was crystal clear to Helena.

Tahlia was surprised by Helena's words, although she felt there was some truth to them. However, Tahlia didn't want to admit it. Sipping her mojito, she changed the subject. "These are delicious, by the way," she said.

Helena examined the drink in her glass. "Thank you, one of my specialties."

Tahlia nodded.

Helena wasn't going to let Tahlia off the hook that fast. "What do you feel your mystery wooden angel would say? After all, she was a magical gift. Perhaps you should ask her for a sign."

"What if she says yes, we just pack up and go?" said Tahlia sarcastically.

"Come on, Tahlia, you love an adventure, don't let your fears taint it; it's up to you to discover the magic. Call Seraphina in; she always comes to you when you need her the most. And you always said the visits from Ivan and Serge bring you clarity."

Tahlia thought, *Why is Helena pushing this, why doesn't she have my back on this?* Inwardly, Tahlia knew that part of her was too scared to see the truth; perhaps it was time to move on, and Helena could see this.

"Tahlia, you have always believed in the magic and miracles of life; it's time to trust again. You can create a life you love."

Tahlia looked at her best friend with an inner knowing, and they smiled at each other; clinking their glasses and allowing the orange skies to bathe them in the setting sun.

On her way home, Tahlia noticed the full moon rising over the horizon of the beach. She stopped to watch it, contemplating what Helena had said: "Finding the magic is up to you."

Tahlia stepped onto the beach, placing her feet in the water's edge, allowing the water to kiss her toes. In the waves, Tahlia saw a mist rising out of the water, and couldn't quite make it out. *It must be the light*, she thought. O*r not, maybe Seraphina had heard us talking about her.* Her magical friend, Seraphina, gracefully moved toward her.

"Hello, Tahlia, isn't the moon lovely," said Seraphina, as if to confirm she was looking at the same moon and wasn't just in Tahlia's imagination. Tahlia made a mental note of how Seraphina's presence always felt calming and reassuring.

"Mike says we are ready to move on," Tahlia clumsily blurted, "he wants us to buy a boat and sail the Mediterranean."

Seraphina looked at her, lovingly, "Are you ready to move on?"

"No, yes…I'm so confused. Part of me says yes, another part doesn't want to let go of what we have. The last two years have been hard enough, now to physically say yes to a new change by choice. Are we mad? Shouldn't we just see what life unfolds?" Tahlia had so many concerns.

Seraphina spoke gently, "My beautiful friend, life *is* unfolding; this idea would not have sparked in your husband's mind if it wasn't part of the unfolding journey. Mike's inspiration is showing him what you both need, and maybe the life you are clinging to isn't the best thing for you anymore. What lies ahead could be incredible, bringing you so much more joy."

Tahlia observed these were almost the same words Helena had used.

"But what if it doesn't, what if it is full of more tragedy? I don't know I could cope with that," Tahlia said.

"Tahlia, you have been able to move through your worst nightmare, finding the strength inside that you never knew existed. That strength is always there for you; it is part of you. You can draw upon it wherever you are."

Tahlia flinched for a moment, remembering Ivan and Serge saying challenges make us stronger.

"Tahlia, our souls want to expand and grow. That is why growth and change are always happening. It's something you can't control. Tahlia, remember it's what you do with the change, how you feel throughout it. Acceptance and peace or resistance and struggle – you have a choice. If you look all around you, life and nature are constantly showing you exactly how life unfolds."

Needing clarity on the jumbled mess of thoughts in her head, Tahlia responded, "Seraphina, I guess Mike needs this, and I know it's his passion. I do love adventure, and Mike always finds a way to lead us to the magic. It's just, how do I tell if it is my heart or head leading me?

Seraphina placed her hand on Tahlia's heart. "You know in your heart what feels right. Does this new life, on the boat, feel expansive?"

Tahlia took a deep breath, "Yes," replied Tahlia feeling her heart pulsing, opening up.

Still, with her hand on Tahlia's heart, Seraphina asked, "Tahlia, take another breath. Now, does staying home feel expansive?"

Tahlia was surprised by her reply. "No. I feel all contracted at the thought, like I'm suffocating."

"There is your answer, my beautiful friend. Always follow your bliss, following what expands your heart. If it contracts your heart, then it's not for you."

Tahlia gazed at the full moon as she allowed Seraphina's wisdom to sink in. When she turned to thank her magical friend, Seraphina was gone. Tahlia's heart was still gently pulsating.

When Tahlia returned home, she found Mike at the kitchen bench on the computer. She leaned in and gave him a big hug. "What are you up to?"

"I was just looking up some boats. Do you want to see?"

Tahlia smiled and pulled out the stool next to him. They cruised through the internet, looking at a variety of sailing boats. Mike knew what he wanted. He was skilled at finding the most photogenic pictures, alluring Tahlia with photos of full sails protruding from white hauls, floating on turquoise blue water, in exotic landscapes, pointing out the inviting decks to laze around on.

Mike carried on his running commentary. "Look at this one, Tahlia; it has a door from the cabin to the front, indoor-outdoor living." Flicking through the pictures of the next boat, "Look, at the modern décor. Everything we need, even a coffee maker, a bed you can walk around." he cheekily nudged Tahlia. "It will be like living in a fancy apartment we can pack up and take anywhere instantly."

Tahlia found herself immersed in his dream.

As they climbed into bed, Mike snuggled in, not pressuring Tahlia, gently saying, "Tahlia, a new life would be wonderful. Imagine sailing with the dolphins, feeling carefree."

Tahlia's passionate love for dolphins and her free spirit liked the sound of that.

Looking Mike in the eyes, she took a deep breath and replied, "Yes, let's do it. I'm up for a new adventure."

Mike was relieved. He had been yearning to do this; he knew it was right for them both.

Lovingly they snuggled into each other's arms, embracing their new dream.

As Tahlia melted into sleep, she saw herself wandering along a marina; it felt like she was in a French coastal village, surrounded by mesmerizing calm turquoise water, cobbled stone streets lined with cafes filled with red, white and blue tablecloths. It was early morning as Tahlia meandered along the marina, a faint smell of lavender lingering in the air. She noticed all types of boats moored alongside each other, some with sailing masts standing tall and proud.

"Well, hello, fancy meeting you here!" Serge was with Ivan waving and walking along the Marina toward her. Tahlia was ecstatic to see them.

"Hi, Tahlia, its beautiful, isn't it? Are you enjoying how peaceful it is here?" said Ivan approaching Tahlia.

Tahlia stopped, taking in the breath-taking stillness and beauty. She could feel peace radiating and vibrating all around her; as she breathed, a familiar sense of calm come over her. *Is this what it will be like on the boat?* she thought, as she looked around, taking in her environment.

"Do either of you know anything about boats?" she burst out, ruining the tranquil moment.

Serge laughed, a big belly laugh echoing out across the water. "Sure do, Madame. I love sailing; the ocean has so many gifts. What would you like to know?"

All of a sudden, Tahlia felt stupid. "My husband, Mike, he wants us to change our lives and go sailing. I don't know much about sailing; I don't even know if I will like it." Tahlia seemed stressed. "I guess I was hoping you could give me some confidence or something."

Serge nudged Ivan, both of them smiling.

"There is a lot of learning on a boat. Tahlia, the only way to gain your confidence is to spend time sailing. I'll let you in on a big secret, Tahlia, you need to go with the flow more than anything," answered Serge. "Life, the ocean, the wind – they all are out of your control. The only thing you can control is how you feel in the moment and how you choose to react in each moment. Trust me; it makes for smoother sailing if you choose to go with the flow rather than struggle and force things."

Tahlia was looking at him a little concerned, knowing how she liked feeling in control. For Tahlia, letting go had been a big lesson with the passing of Jayden and Sierra, but a part of her still wanted to feel in control.

As if reading Tahlia's thoughts, Ivan said, "It's not always easy to go with the flow, Tahlia. We often think we know best and sometimes find ourselves resisting and struggling, trying to control the environment."

Serge laughed again. "Isn't that the truth. However, one thing with water and boats: there is always a flow. The same goes for life."

Tahlia gazed out over the marina, "Serge, is there a secret to going with the flow?"

"When you are in the flow, it feels peaceful and calm inside, like a gentle knowing all is well. This serene, happy feeling exists while you are immersed in what you are doing." Serge paused, looking at the water. "Tahlia, see the water running out there?" he said, pointing to the current. "Imagine you wanted to swim to the big blue sailing boat in the middle. If you jumped into the water, swimming, or even just floating, the flow of the current would take you there in no time. However, if the tide were coming in, you would have to use extra effort to swim against the current to get to the boat. It would be a struggle and feel like you are swimming forever."

"Personally, for me, no flow, no go. I would avoid the tough swim and head off to enjoy a cold beer while I waited for the tide to change," he said, laughing and rubbing his beer belly.

They all joined in laughing.

Tahlia woke, loving her visits with Serge and Ivan; it felt so real, even if they were in her imagination...what did it matter? She was thankful and looked forward to Ivan and Serge showing up because the days following always seemed to be filled with amazing flow and clarity.

∞ 22 ∞

LETTING GO

HELENA AND HER husband were thrilled for Mike and Tahlia.

"This will be the adventure of a lifetime," said Helena. "I can't wait to join you on the boat for a few cocktails."

Both Helena and Tahlia knew they would miss each other dearly, yet in their hearts, they knew this adventure had to happen.

Life changed rapidly from that moment.

Tahlia and Mike consulted with real-estate agents, putting their newly renovated house on the market. They decided it best to have a garage sale. *What a mammoth effort this would be,* Tahlia thought, a little overwhelmed. *Oh, well, let's start with the small steps.*

In her spare time, Tahlia worked her way through culling everything.

Sifting through her wardrobe and picking up a pair of high heels, Tahlia thought, *who knew a woman could own so many shoes? Guess I won't be needing those on the boat.* She quickly placed them and four other pairs in a for-sale pile.

Tahlia looked through their library of books; she loved her books and the thought of discarding them was painful. Maybe she could find a good charity for them to go to, that would make her feel good. *It's kind of liberating*, thought Tahlia as she went through each section at a time.

Mike had loads of tools in the garage along with all the camping gear, which seemed just as hard as Tahlia's books to cull.

Every day, Tahlia would feel different layers of fear arise, usually in moments of being tired or stressed, her thoughts distracting her from her mission. She did her best to embrace the task at hand, practicing going with the flow. "No flow, no go," she told herself, remembering Serge's explanation of swimming with the current. Tahlia knew too well how hard it was swimming upstream. Following the flow, Tahlia was amazed at how quickly everything slotted into place.

Mike and Tahlia had already let go of a lot of Jayden and Sierra's things, but they still had two large boxes full of their favorite memories from the twins. Neither Mike nor Tahlia wanted to open the boxes, nor did they know what to do with them, continually moving the boxes from one side of the garage to the other. Eventually, they decided they would put Sierra and Jayden's boxes in storage. Throughout the culling process, Mike and Tahlia had already decided to hire a small storage shed for the things they valued and wanted to hang onto.

Everything was flowing fast; they attracted a buyer for the house who even wanted to purchase all their furniture. Stoked at how convenient this was, Mike and Tahlia felt a huge relief.

That night at dinner, Tahlia casually asked Mike, "What's our next step?"

Mike eagerly told Tahlia, "I've been looking online, and believe I've found the perfect boat, which I think you will love. I feel it would be worth me taking a trip to Europe to check it out."

Tahlia felt a strange feeling in the pit of her stomach. What was this feeling? Fear, or excitement? She wasn't sure.

"Do you want me to come with you?" she asked, hesitantly.

"I was thinking it might be best if you stay here and continue to clear things out."

Tahlia's eyes quickly scanned Mike's face. *He can't possibly be serious*, she thought in panic. If Tahlia stayed home, it would be the first time she would be alone without Mike, without anyone.

The strange feeling in her stomach formed a lump in her throat, Tahlia felt uneasy, squirming in her chair.

"Are you sure? Don't you want me to see the boat too?" she asked, pushing the food on her plate around with her fork as if pushing the uncomfortable feelings back down.

"It will be a quick trip, Tahlia, and I'll probably have to look at quite a few boats in different places," Mike replied, noticing how restless Tahlia was acting. He could feel that the atmosphere between them had suddenly become tense.

"Tahlia, I honestly feel it's more productive and better to save the airfare. It won't be for long, I promise. I can always Facetime you when I am there, so you see the boat." Mike did his best to convince her. "

Tahlia looked at Mike; she could see he was excited. She wanted to believe and trust in his decision, a part of her knowing he was right, but the lump in her throat was threatening to explode.

"What if something horrible happens to you?" she blurted out, voicing her fear, as a tear slid down her cheek.

Mike could see Tahlia was scared; he was, too. However, his excitement of their dream coming true helped him focus. Leaning over, Mike handed her a napkin to wipe her tears.

"I know it will feel weird being apart, and I will miss you, Tahlia, but who knows, the way everything is panning out so easily, this first boat might be the one? Tahlia, I'll be back before you know it," he added, trying to soften her discomfort.

Tahlia nodded, not wanting to make Mike feel bad. She knew she would have to let him go and deal with this fear of being apart.

Seraphina's words rang in her ears, "Tahlia, this pathway of change will always lead to something new, your role is to accept the change, surrender into it, and flow peacefully along the journey. In that process, you will feel joy."

That night they booked Mike's trip. Tahlia made a list of things to do that would keep her busy, thinking, *who knows where this will lead?* She was both scared and excited.

***

Mike was shaking Tahlia awake. "Wake up, Honey, time to take me to the airport, I don't want to be late."

Tahlia jumped up quickly, racing around, pulling on some jeans and a T-shirt. Mike was packed and ready to go, coffee in hand. He smiled at his wife racing around, feeling how much he loved her.

Tahlia drove Mike to the airport in uneasy silence. Both were consumed in thinking about this being the first time they would be spending a week apart since Jayden and Sierra's death. It felt strange and uncomfortable; they had become each other's rock and best friend clinging to each other's presence for their inner strength.

"I'm going to miss you, Mike," said Tahlia, changing the awkward silence.

"Ditto, Tahlia, it's odd I know, but I'm already counting the hours until I am in your arms again." He smiled at her, affectionately resting his hand on her leg.

Tahlia pulled up in the drop-off zone. They both got out of the car for one last loving embrace, lingering in the hug, almost as if it would be the last time.

Tahlia looked Mike in the eyes, for that split-second recognizing those alluring blue eyes that had promised her so much fun and freedom. "Love you," she said, burying her head in the comfort of his chest, disguising her tears.

Mike broke their embrace, clearing his throat. "I have to go now, Tahlia. I love you to the moon and back," he said swiftly, turning before she saw the tears in his eyes.

Tahlia watched Mike walk into the terminal, disappearing into the expansive sea of other travelers.

Tahlia cried for the entire drive home, a piece of her heart feeling abandoned and lonely; uncertain of what lay ahead, acknowledging their life was now in the midst of a new change, once again.

∞ 23 ∞

ACTING ON INSPIRATION

MIKE GOT OFF the plane in Marseille, a bustling city and port in southern France. He relaxed into the thirty-five-minute taxi ride, admiring the French countryside as the taxi weaved its way around the hills down into the quaint town of Cassis.

Arriving at the Port de Cassis, Mike paid the taxi driver and headed straight toward the Marina office.

A stocky, colorful character was there to meet him, "Bonjour, puis-je vous aider."

"Pardon, in English," said Mike, a little embarrassed he had not brushed up on his French.

"Hi, I'm Serge. Can I help you?"

"Hello, I'm Mike. I have an appointment to look at some boats for sale," he said, showing Serge the pictures on his phone and his booking.

"Oui, this one she is a beauty, I'll take you there now," remarked Serge.

They strolled along the Marina, Mike taking it all in, the blue water, colorful mountainous landscape, the boats.

Serge indicated that Mike should step aboard the boat in front of them. Mike enthusiastically did so, his excitement fading rather quickly, realizing the boat looked much better in the online photos than in real life.

"Serge, it's not quite what we are after," said Mike, trying not to sound discouraged. Flicking through pictures on his phone Mike was grateful he had a backup plan. "Can I look at these others?"

Serge happily showed Mike around a few other boats for sale. The boats were either too small, too old, or not quite the standard he had in mind to convince Tahlia.

"Voila, what do you think?" claimed Serge, opening his hands in a grand gesture as he was showing Mike the last boat in his fleet.

"Serge, I'm sorry, I have to be honest, it's not the one for us," Mike replied, looking around disappointed. "Thank you for showing me what you have for sale but, none of them feel right. My wife, she hasn't sailed a lot, and I want her to feel comfortable and love it."

"I agree, boats are like women, you must get the one that feels right," laughed Serge.

Mike chuckled; Serge was a fun character and he liked his energy. They walked back to the Marina office, sharing sailing stories and discussing some of the features that would make a sailing catamaran the best new home for Mike and Tahlia. Mike noted how comfortable he felt with Serge. It was as if he understood exactly everything Tahlia and Mike needed.

Tired and weary from traveling, Mike collected his bag from the office, shaking Serge's hand, "Thank you, Serge. I'd appreciate you letting me know if you hear of any other sailing boats in the area that would fit our style. I'm staying at the Hotel Le Cassiden, just down there on the corner," added Mike, pointing down the village street.

Serge nodded as he returned to his desk, opening his computer. "I will see if I can find your boat, Monsieur Mike, Au revoir."

Mike strolled toward Hotel Le Cassiden. The town of Cassis appeared to be a charming little village; *Tahlia would like it here,* he thought.

Settling into his room, Mike began feeling a little disheartened; he wished Tahlia was with him. He needed to hear her voice.

Mike rang home, "Hi, Tahlia."

"Mike, it's so good to hear your voice. How is boat-hunting going?" Tahlia was excited to be speaking with Mike.

"Well, let's just say out of all the boats I saw none were right, most appeared more alluring in the online photos than in person." Mike paused, "Honestly, Tahlia, I'm not sure this is the right thing. I had imagined us living on a catamaran with features you love, but none seem to match up to our standards."

"Oh, Mike, you've only seen a few, and I'm sure you'll find the right one. You have that natural ability to be drawn to what we need," Tahlia added reassuringly.

Mike wasn't so sure, changing the subject he asked, "How are you, Tahlia? How is everything at home?"

"All good, I sold a few more items on swap-and-buy today."

"Wow, Tahlia, that's great! You're doing a fabulous job at moving us forward. Anything else happening?" Mike wanted to keep her talking; he realized how much he missed having Tahlia beside him.

"No, not really, I'm sure the south of France is far more exciting," she laughed into the phone. "Is it pretty there?"

"Yes, it's gorgeous, Tahlia. You would love it here." Mike's voice trailed off, feeling lonely, desperately wishing she were with him.

Picking up a change in Mike's energy, Tahlia was concerned, "You okay, Mike?"

There was a slight pause before Mike responded, as he didn't want Tahlia to get upset, "I'm just exhausted from the traveling and boat hunting. Tahlia, I better go. I'll call you tomorrow. Love you."

"Love you, too," replied Tahlia with a smile.

As Mike hung up, he reclined back on the big bed, sinking into the silky soft French sheets, falling asleep and dreaming he was holding Tahlia in his arms.

***

Opening the curtains to a beautiful day, Mike peered out his window, overlooking a cobblestone street leading to the Marina, out into the Mediterranean sea. Mike could feel the tantalizing body of water calling him. He stood there, breathing it all in.

Venturing downstairs for breakfast, Mike found a cute little café attached to the hotel. Choosing to sit outside, Mike was enjoying a warm croissant when the hotel receptionist came over and handed him a note.

"For you, Monsieur Mike," she said, giving him a neatly folded piece of paper.

Mike unfolded the paper:

> *Monsieur Mike*
> *Meet me at the Mariana office at 11 am*
> **à bientôt** *Serge*

Mike glanced at his watch, registering it was 10.00 am. Smiling to himself, he had a good feeling about this.

Basking in a leisurely breakfast, Mike relaxed into the ambience of the café, soaking up the sun and the laid-back French lifestyle. He enjoyed seeing the fishermen excited with their catch of the day, the locals carrying their baguettes, the hum of the French language all around him.

Checking his watch, Mike grabbed his backpack and headed to the Marina.

Approaching the Marina office, Mike noticed another man was talking in French with Serge.

Serge looked up, waving, "Bonjour, Monsieur Mike."

Even though Serge spoke perfect English, he thought it was fun to greet Mike in French.

"Ivan, this is Mike," Serge moved aside as Ivan shook Mike's hand.

"Mike, tell my friend Ivan, this catamaran you want to buy, who is it for; someone special?" prompted Serge.

"My wife Tahlia, she is my best friend and love of my life," Mike said affectionately. "We are looking for a sea change." Mike found himself wanting to explain. "A couple of years ago, our twins, Jayden and Sierra, they died in a bad car accident." Mike hesitated for a moment before continuing, "Tahlia and I have been through hell and back. I want us to have a fresh start, a new chapter of our lives." Mike couldn't believe he was telling two strangers this.

"I'm sorry for your loss," said Ivan, moved by Mike's story. "You are blessed to have each other."

"Yes, we are," replied Mike, sensing a slight sadness in Ivan's voice.

"Mike, are you ready for an adventure? I think we have the perfect boat for you," said Serge, winking at Ivan.

Serge motioned for Mike to enter the car, "We have a short drive to your boat, Monsieur. I hope you like winding roads."

Mike smiled at Serge's cheekiness.

"Mike, have you heard of the Calanques? You must see them; they are magnificently fascinating inlets within the Parc National," said Ivan, climbing into the back seat.

The drive was impressive: old French-style houses with steeply sloping roofs, blue painted wooden shutters, all perched next to the narrow roads winding around the cliffs, with views of the expansive ocean glistening in the sunlight. Mikes' senses took it all in.

Arriving at the Port of Calanques de Cassis, Mike was in awe at the number of boats. Some anchored in the middle, and hundreds moored next to each other on the wooden docks. Boat after boat after boat, bobbing on the pristine water. Sail stays, making a clinking sound in the slight breeze next to rocky cliffs jutting into the ocean.

The three men strolled along the wooden dock, admiring the yachts and catamarans. Serge and Ivan stopped about halfway along the jetty.

"Mike, I think you will love this one," said Serge stepping aboard a white catamaran in front of them.

Ivan ushered Mike on board.

From the moment Mike stepped aboard, something felt different about this boat. Mike could feel an excited feeling in his stomach. As Mike explored the catamaran, he noticed an elevated sense of joy. Inside, the cabins seemed perfect; everything was tastefully decorated. The master cabin had a big bed you could walk around and a lovely ensuite. He knew Tahlia would want to add her style, but it was pretty good already. The engine was clean, almost like new. The boat even had a water-making system, so many features Mike had dreamt of.

Mike was getting more excited by the minute. He walked to the front deck, where Ivan and Serge were chatting.

"What do you think?" asked Serge.

"I like it," replied Mike. "Seems to have everything we want. I love the style. How does she sail?"

"Like an eagle soaring," said Ivan rather quickly.

"Have you sailed her, Ivan?" asked Mike questionably.

Serge was grinning at Ivan as if there were some kind of joke.

"You could say that," nodded Ivan.

"This is Ivan's boat," added Serge.

Mike was curious, "Really, it's lovely. Is it for sale?"

"Yes, I'm ready to see her go to a good owner, it's time."

Mike was relieved, as he had silently fallen in love with the catamaran.

"Would you like to head out for a quick sail?" offered Ivan.

"Definitely," Mike nodded.

Mike was thrilled as the three of them sailed in the gentle breeze, making their way out through the spectacular Calanques inlet, sailing on the French Mediterranean. Mike loved how well the boat handled; she looked magnificent with the sails up. Tacking around Pointe D'en Vau, they navigated their way into Calanque D'en Vau. The bay housed a small beach surrounded by rock walls; the water was so clear you could see the floor of the ocean. Mike was beaming with happiness; the sailing was fun, the company good and the scenery spectacular, it was everything he had imagined.

As they drove back into the village of Cassis, Mike was still buzzing from the excitement and could feel the sensation of joy vibrating through his whole body. He gazed out the window, thinking about the boat, and how everything seemed perfect. The price was the only twist – a little more than they had budgeted. What could he do to create this dream come true?

Ivan and Serge took Mike to their favorite local restaurant for lunch. All three were joking and laughing; Mike captivated by their stories.

Ivan was sharing some of his adventures on the boat. "I remember once Joyful Adventures was caught in a big wind gust…."

"Joyful Adventures?" interrupted Mike.

"Yes, that's her name, the boat," said Ivan.

"You're kidding me," Mike was stunned. *How could that be? Tahlia is not going to believe this; he had found a boat named Joyful Adventures.* Mike began thinking about the ornament he had crafted out of the twins' favorite toys and how those words had kept coming to him.

"If you don't like the name, you are welcome to change it," said Ivan, a little confused with Mike's reaction.

Serge piped up, "Of course, us true men of the sea believe it is bad luck to change the name of a boat."

"No, no, I love the name. My wife, she has something special called Joyful Adventures, back at home. I think she will be pleasantly surprised," said Mike, dismissing the coincidence.

The stories continued, Mike, enjoying the friendly banter between Serge and Ivan.

As they finished lunch and coffee came, Ivan looked at Mike, "I have been thinking Mike, if you love Joyful Adventures and think that your wife would like her too, I would be happy to strike a deal. If you pay three-quarters upfront, you can have full use of the boat, and we both would share the ownership papers until you pay the remainder of the sum owed within the next six-to-twelve months."

Mike was astounded. From what he knew, no one ever did deals like this with boats.

"Ivan, that's an incredible offer, thank you." Mike had a grin from ear to ear. "I'm very keen on it, but I have to run it past my wife and get back to you."

"Certainly, Mike."

They exchanged a gentleman's handshake. Mike noticed a strange pulsating energy in his hand, moving up his arm all over his body. It felt as if Ivan had passed some sort of electrical current to Mike.

They said their good-bye's, Ivan and Serge sauntering back to the Marina office. Mike was full of excitement, floating on cloud nine as he made his way back to hotel Le Cassiden. Not only had Mike manifested finding a boat called Joyful Adventures, now the owner was happy to let him pay it off. He couldn't wait to ring Tahlia.

Ring ring, ring ring....

"Hello, hello, is that you, Mike?" Tahlia could hear a slight delay in the connection.

"Tahlia, I've found it. I've found the perfect boat for us. It is ten times better than any of the ones I showed you on the internet. It's got everything we need, and she sails beautifully." Mike couldn't contain his excitement, spilling it all out, "I met these two guys – Ivan and Serge –, and they are happy to let us purchase Ivan's catamaran for three-quarters upfront and pay it off in next six-to-twelve months. The deal is incredible!"

Tahlia's attention instantly heightened; did she hear correctly? "Hang on a minute, Mike, slow down. You met two guys named Ivan and Serge?"

"Yeah, they are funny guys, very hospitable. Anyway, it was, still is, Ivan's boat and he wants it to go to a good owner. Ivan seems to like me; he thinks we might be the best people for the boat."

Tahlia was speechless, trying to absorb it all.

"On top of that, you are not going to believe what the name of the boat is." Mike paused a moment: "Joyful Adventures."

"Are you for real?" Tahlia shrieked through the phone "No way!"

"Yes, way, I'm serious. Tahlia, this boat is meant to be."

Both of them burst into tears, tears of joy.

"Tahlia, I'll send the photos through now, so you can check her out." Mike was buzzing.

"Mike, if you believe this is the best boat for us, you know I totally trust your opinion."

"Tahlia, I know you will love it – and all the wonderful adventures we can go on."

"Sounds to me, Mike, that you've got a boat to buy. Off you go," Tahlia said, smiling to herself, acknowledging how good it was to hear her husband so happy.

Mike was ecstatic; he hadn't felt this much joy in a very long time.

Tahlia got off the phone, totally flabbergasted. *What were the chances that Mike would run into two men named Ivan and Serge, and on top of that, they had a catamaran to sell called Joyful Adventures?* She raced into the bedroom to see if her mystery angel was still on the bedside table. Expecting it to be gone or doing something mystical, like floating in mid-air, Tahlia found the angel where she had left it. Tahlia picked up the wooden angel, slowly tracing her fingers across its praying hands. Looking into the cherub's eyes, Tahlia felt an inner knowing that something was divinely guiding them. Life suddenly seemed to have a miraculous flow.

Tahlia immediately rang Helena and told her the news.

"Can you believe it, Helena? It's incredible!" Tahlia was beside herself with what was unfolding.

"That's what you and I love about the magic of life, Tahlia; it's full of many surprises and coincidences." Helena was riding the wave of Tahlia's excitement, "Let's get you packing and selling off the last of everything. You've got a new adventure that awaits."

***

Helena and Tahlia organized a big garage sale, creating signs, setting up tables, displaying the items for sale. Helena baked cookies to give out to everyone, as she believed the best way to a successful sale was through a happy tummy. People arrived, finding treasures and items they needed with ease. Everything sold fast.

Mike had stayed an extra few days in Cassis to finalize every-thing with Ivan and Serge. When he returned, Mike was surprised at how fast everything was moving. Tahlia had sold most things and packed nearly all of what they wanted to keep. He noticed the Joyful Adventures ornament still sitting on the sideboard. Mike picked it up, reflecting on when he had made it out of the twin's favorite toys.

"What do we do with this?" softly asked Mike.

"I'm not sure, we could take it, or maybe we can leave it with our parents, to take care of it for us," suggested Tahlia.

"I feel we need to take the ornament; it was their favorite," Mike's voice trailed off, the enormity of the change upon them had suddenly hit him.

"Are we doing the right thing, Tahlia? Our life is here, everyone we love, our memories." Mike allowed the tears to flow.

Tahlia gently snuggled into his back, her arms wrapped around his chest, "I understand Mike, but I believe it is time for us to create new memories, a new life together. I know that's what the twins would want." She felt him lean back into her, surrendering.

"We can do this. I know we can. It's scary, and it's exciting. Mike, in your words, it's time."

Mike turned and looked into her sweet reassuring eyes.

"Yes, it is time, Tahlia," he whispered as gentle tears flowed down their faces, both releasing their fears.

∞ 24 ∞

EMBARKING ON A NEW LIFE

THE DAY ARRIVED. Everyone was fan-faring Mike and Tahlia off at the airport, sharing food and drinks, clinking glasses, and cheering as if it were a big Greek wedding. The atmosphere was full of excitement, tears, and laughter – a roller-coaster of emotions. Helena was holding tight onto Tahlia, not wanting to let her go.

"I'm going to miss you, my friend," Tahlia managed between her tears.

"Thank goodness for social media; you'll see me all the time! We will always be connected," Helena joked between her tears. "Besides, you will be busy organizing the local cuisine, deck chairs, and alcohol for our sunset cocktails."

Laughing, the two friends shared a loving embrace.

Mike took Tahlia's hand, signaling they should go.

"Thank you, everyone, we love you and can't wait to see you on our new boat, floating around the Mediterranean. Make sure you come and join us!"

Everyone cheered, watching as Mike and Tahlia headed off. Tahlia patted her backpack, checking that her mystery angel was still with her. She had decided to place the mystery angel in her onboard luggage, as it was her way of feeling connected, ensuring all was still okay as they walked into uncertainty.

Despite the roller-coaster of emotions flowing through her, Tahlia could feel that both Mike and she believed this adventure was meant to be.

"Boarding now," ushered a flight attendant.

Mike and Tahlia looked at each other, holding hands for inner strength, walking onto the plane, into a new chapter of their lives.

They found their seats and settled in. Tahlia was exhausted, emotionally and physically, from the build-up of leaving. She rested her head on Mike's shoulder and fell into a deep sleep on the plane.

On the inner side of her eyelids, she met Ivan and Serge sitting in Ivan's living room, playing cards.

"Hey, hey, careful sneaking up on us like that, you'll give two old men a heart attack," Serge laughed.

Tahlia always loved Serge's friendly welcome banter.

"Tahlia, how are you?" Ivan welcomed her to sit and join them.

Tahlia found herself childishly blurting, "I'm scared and excited. We bought the boat, packed up everything, left everyone and everything we know."

Ivan and Serge raised an eyebrow "Wow, that's a mouthful Tahlia, what a brave change," said Ivan.

"Brave, I'm not so sure, I have no idea what we have done. All I know is that we are starting a new chapter of our life." Tahlia felt somewhat relieved, having voiced it out loud to the two men.

"Last time we saw you, Tahlia, you wanted to know about the flow. "I'm curious, did you find the flow?" smiled Serge.

"Yes, everything seemed to happen so quickly. It was incredible, like we were being divinely guided or helped along the way."

"May I ask, then, why do you feel scared?" said Ivan.

"Ivan, I'm so out of my comfort zone. I hardly know anything about boats. There is so much unknown, and out of my control, it frightens me," replied Tahlia, her anxiety building.

"Tahlia, remember the only thing you have control over is how you choose to flow with the change. Do your best to intend to feel peace and joy, seeing beauty in every moment, surrendering into it," said Ivan in a calming voice.

"I've been practicing really hard, and it's not always easy. Every time I think about the enormity of what we have done, I get overwhelmed. My brain starts filling me with all the fearful what-ifs," she sighed. "I try to come back to the moment, to accept this is our new life. I have glimpses of joy and excitement. I'm not sure I'm doing it right," said a troubled Tahlia, shaking her head.

"Tahlia, relax," laughed Serge, "Life is fun, the universe wants you to play and enjoy yourself, sometimes we have to let go and trust completely."

"Remember to breathe, Tahlia, breathe." Ivan's words drifted off.

Tahlia was pulled out of her vision, hearing the loud announcement, "Ladies and gentlemen, we are commencing our descent, please fasten your seatbelts, secure your tray tables, and ensure your hand luggage is securely stowed."

Slightly disorientated, Tahlia couldn't believe they were already touching down in Paris. One more quick flight, and they would be in Marseille.

It was a tight connection; Mike and Tahlia found their way to the next boarding gate. Tahlia felt she was in a daze: must be jet lag, the exhaustion, everything all piled up. She was unable to make sense of her thoughts or vision.

Boarding the flight, Mike let Tahlia have the window seat, as he wanted her to see the view. The plane began flying at altitude, Tahlia gazed blankly out the window – and suddenly the twins appeared, playing on big white fluffy clouds. They were laughing, having so much fun, cloud surfing. Jayden would jump from one to the other, chasing Sierra as she fell through down to the next level. Both trusting the clouds would catch them, Tahlia watched fondly.

Sierra waved, catching Tahlia's eye, "Mum, come and play; it's so much fun."

Jayden stopped to look around at Tahlia, "Watch this, mum," he said as he plummeted through two layers of clouds.

Tahlia found herself gasping and leaned closer to the window to see if he landed. Jayden was lying on his back in fits of laughter, surrounded by white fluffiness, the soft clouds reminding Tahlia of spun fairy floss. Tahlia turned to Mike to see if he could see the twins playing. Mike's eyelids were firmly closed, his head leaning to one side. He looked so peaceful.

Tahlia turned back to the window, Jayden and Sierra were waving at her, blowing kisses, mouthing, "We love you both."

Tahlia's view of the twins faded as the plane descended below the clouds. In their place, Tahlia saw the sparkling blue waters of the Mediterranean, luring her in.

Reflecting on the empty-nesters blog she had read by M, Tahlia thought, *M, the author, had been right, no one shows us what the next chapter should be. It's up to me to dust off my dreams and create a new chapter worth living for.*

Mike awoke from his deep sleep as the plane touched down. Gently kissing Tahlia on the cheek, he whispered: "Here we go, Tahlia, a whole new adventure."

They maneuvered through customs, collecting their bags. It dawned on Tahlia as she looked at her luggage; packed into these four suitcases was their whole life. How had they managed to cull it all?

As they cleared immigration, Mike's voice interrupted her train of thought.

"The previous owners emailed me to say they have sent a car to pick us up," said Mike looking for their names among the drivers holding up placards.

He spotted their names, Mike and Tahlia, with a little sailing boat drawn after it. "Oui, that's us," Mike nodded, motioning to the driver.

The thirty-five-minute drive from Marseille into Cassis seemed to take forever. Tahlia was tired and fidgety. She was over all the traveling and just wanted to be there.

"Tahlia, look, a rainbow!" exclaimed Mike. "That's good luck, isn't it?"

Tahlia nodded, remembering her grandfather had taught her rainbows were giant slippery slides for angels and fairies. As they slide down, the angels and fairies would spread magic, and good luck. Tahlia's grandfather had such a creative imagination, and Tahlia loved envisaging the fun the fairies and angels would have on the rainbow. The memory made Tahlia smile.

As the car made its way, winding down into the village of Cassis, Mike asked the driver to take the scenic route. He had pre-organized with Ivan and Serge to moor Joyful Adventures at Cassis Marina. Mike wanted Tahlia to settle in and get a feel for the French village life before he showed her the Calanques. He intended to surprise Tahlia and sail her over to the Port of Calanques de Cassis once they got their sea legs so that she could take in all its beauty.

Tahlia's senses came alive as she saw the village for the first time. "Mike, check out all the cobblestone alleyways. All those pretty lavender flowers."

Tahlia marveled at the scenes in front of her. The quaint harbor lined with pastel buildings, sidewalk cafes, and restaurants bubbling with people. Tahlia's excitement kicked in.

"Look, Mike, there is even a castle on the hill! Ooh, I can't wait to explore."

He smiled at her enthusiasm as she grabbed his hand.

Arriving at the Port, the driver helped them unload. Tahlia stepped out of the car, taking it all in.

"Come on, Tahlia, this way." Mike began wheeling his bags towards the arm where Joyful Adventures was moored.

Tahlia followed close behind; thankful her luggage had wheels. "Mike, when will I get to meet Ivan and Serge?"

"Soon enough," said Mike, stopping at the gangplank of their new boat. He leaned in and gave her a big hug, "Tahlia, meet Joyful Adventures – our new home."

As she looked up, Tahlia saw Ivan and Serge standing on the back of the catamaran, waiting to welcome them. She shook her head vigorously, thinking now isn't the time for a vision.

"Bonjour, Monsieur Mike, and Madame Tahlia, Bienvenu, welcome," Ivan and Segre called, waving to them. Mike smiled, stepping onto the boat.

Tahlia stood frozen in disbelief. *It can't be Ivan and Serge; they never spoke French to me in my visions. I'm seeing things.*

"Tahlia, are you coming?" asked Mike breaking Tahlia out of her frozen trance.

Ivan stepped forward, introducing himself with a wink, "Ivan, it's a pleasure to meet you, Tahlia."

Tahlia was dumbfounded.

Serge, his usual colorful character with a big belly laugh, stretched his hand out to shake hers: "I'm Serge, welcome to France."

How could it be? Tahlia was speechless.

"Come on, Tahlia, I'll show you around," said Mike.

Tahlia walked through the boat half in a daze, her body tingling with a strange feeling. It was everything Mike had described.

"Voilà, this is our love-making side of the boat," Mike affectionately escorted Tahlia into the master cabin.

"Do you love it?" He couldn't wait for her answer.

Tahlia gave Mike a big hug. "Yes, I love it, Mike. I love you."

He responded by kissing and pushing her slightly, so she landed on the bed.

"I feel like we will have some fun times on Joyful Adventures," Mike grinned, both of them giggling like teenagers.

"But for now, let's join Ivan and Serge on the deck," Mike said, breaking their embrace.

As Mike got up to leave, Tahlia grabbed his hand, "Mike, did you know Ivan and Serge before you came to find the boat?"

"No, of course not, how could I have known them?" he replied.

Tahlia was perplexed but didn't want to show it.

"Okay then, I'll be up in a minute; I just need to get myself together," Tahlia responded.

"Don't be long, Tahlia. I believe Ivan and Serge have a little welcome celebration planned."

Tahlia placed her backpack on the bed beside where she sat, pinching her skin to see if this was real.

Reaching into her backpack, Tahlia pulled out the mystery angel, carefully unwrapping it, scanning over the angel, looking for a clue.

"How can all this be?" she said to the wooden cherub, half expecting to see Seraphina. Lost in the silence of the moment, Tahlia took a deep breath waiting for an answer. All she heard was laughter coming from the deck above. Tahlia took one last look at the mystery angel and placed her on the bed, gently tapping the angels' heart with a kiss for good luck. Tahlia made her way up to the deck.

Ivan and Serge had set up a small celebration of canapés and champagne.

Popping the champagne, Serge yelled, "Voila," filling their glasses.

Together they raised their glasses, clinking them together in one big cheer: "Santé, Cheers."

Their jovial voices echoed across the water.

Tahlia decided to enjoy the moment and not ask questions, even though she was still perplexed. Tahlia had a strange feeling this whole thing had been divinely orchestrated, way beyond her imagining or reasoning.

Watching the sunset, hearing their laughter drift off into the horizon, Tahlia knew from the sensation she was feeling, this was meant to be. All the angst of leaving everything behind felt like a distance memory. She felt a beautiful calm and peace come over her, welcoming in the new life they had created.

∞ 25 ∞
LIFE CAN TRULY BE MAGICAL

MIKE AND TAHLIA spent the first few days setting up their new home on the catamaran. Wandering into the village for supplies, Tahlia bought a couple of lovely furnishings, a few cushions for the sun lounges, and some new French sheets that felt silky soft. She enjoyed rummaging through the local boutiques and stores, getting acquainted with the locals.

Ivan showed Mike all the mechanical ins and outs of Joyful Adventures. Ivan, Serge, and Mike had great fun teaching Tahlia about living on a boat and the names of certain things, such as galley instead of kitchen and the head, being the toilet. Tahlia took it all in her stride, doing her best to go with the flow. She enjoyed having Ivan and Serge around, helping them to settle in.

Tahlia still had not experienced sailing on Joyful Adventures. Mike was waiting for the perfect day to introduce Tahlia to the magic of sailing the Calanques. He wanted it to be special.

Mike was busy working on the foredeck of the boat when Tahlia called to him. "Mike, I'm heading into the village to explore, do you want anything?"

"No, I'm good. Unless you want to bring back one of those delicious French vanilla slices for us to share."

Tahlia smiled as she and Mike had fallen in love with the pastries. She kissed him and headed off. Mike was happy that Tahlia felt comfortable exploring the village on her own, that's one of the things he loved about her, her sense of adventure and adaptability.

Tahlia had learned that Ivan and Serge lived in the village, no more visiting them in her dreams as they were here, in reality. She still couldn't believe it and had questions for them, even for Seraphina, her mystery angel.

Tahlia decided to try and find Ivan's home. She had his address and was following directions on Google maps. As Tahlia rounded the corner and entered the street, it all felt familiar. She recognized the cobblestone path leading to a small stone house with painted blue shutters, feeling a strong sense of déjà vu. Tahlia knocked on the door. It felt strange to knock. Usually, Tahlia was mysteriously transported into Ivan's living room.

Ivan opened the door, "Bonjour, Tahlia, nice to see you. Come in," He said, extending his palm and welcoming her into his home.

Tahlia noticed that it looked exactly the same as her visitations with him. The same cozy armchair that Ivan would sit on, all his eclectic artifacts from his travels, a familiar smell of cinnamon. Even the delicately carved wooden box, which held his daughter's letter, was sitting on the table next to his chair.

"Please, Tahlia, have a seat," said Ivan.

Tahlia sat on the sofa; in the same place she always did.

"How are you enjoying Cassis?"

"I love it, Ivan, I feel so comfortable in this little town."

"I'm glad, Tahlia, it's a big change for you and Mike." Ivan looked Tahlia directly in the eyes; she felt as if he knew everything.

"Now, would you like something to drink, perhaps water or tea?" offered Ivan.

She tried answering in French, "Aqua, S'il vous plait."

"Très bien, Tahlia, very good. Water it is," smiled Ivan.

As Ivan disappeared into the kitchen, Tahlia couldn't help but wonder, *Are you real or not? What do I say?* Part of her didn't want to ruin the magic, the mystery. Ivan and Serge had been so kind to her. She didn't know how to approach the subject.

"Ivan, do you believe in magic?" she casually asked as he handed her the glass of water.

"Magic, Tahlia, it's a mystery to me. What's real, what's not, this world is full of many illusions."

Tahlia couldn't help her words from spilling out. "Then Ivan, what's the explanation, of my having been here before. You know I've spent time with you and Serge in this lounge room, all the guidance you have given me, the letter from your daughter...." She trailed off.

"Tahlia, some things in life are unexplainable. Perhaps many lives and worlds exist at the same time." Ivan shrugged his shoulders, "We're all made up of energy, floating around in space and time. Anything is possible, that is the intrigue and fascination of life."

Ivan took a breath, reflecting before continuing, "All I know is that you appeared on my path, shivering, cold, and in a bad way. Now look...you are here, happy and healthy. It's not my role to question life; I have learned to trust and unfold with it. Besides, sometimes the not knowing makes life seem more magical and fun."

Tahlia knew from Ivan's comments that she would never fully understand how all those visions occurred or how they ended up meeting in real life. One thing she knew for certain was that having Ivan and Serge living here in France reassured her that she was on the right path. Tahlia decided to let go of needing an answer, and enjoyed the afternoon chatting, laughing, taking in Ivan's wisdom.

As she got up to leave, Tahlia noticed on the mantelpiece a small carved wooden angel. Tahlia walked over toward the angel, a little stunned, as it looked like a mini version of her mystery angel. "May I?" she said, reaching out to pick it up.

Ivan nodded his head.

"She is beautiful, where did you get her?" Tahlia could feel the angel pulsing in her hands.

"She was a gift; my grandmother carved it for me."

"Your grandmother carved this? How exquisite, she must have been very talented." Tahlia was in awe at how similar it looked and felt to hers.

"Yes," Ivan said fondly, "she was very creative. Grandma would carve by hand at night. She enjoyed the stillness and peace when everyone was in bed. Grandma would recite her prayers, pouring them into the angel, as she carved."

Tahlia noticed Ivan spoke very gently when reflecting upon his grandmother.

"That angel helped me through my wife's death and my daughter's suicide. It brought me great peace, soothing my heart."

"It feels very precious, Ivan." Tahlia reverently placed the angel back on the mantelpiece, feeling overwhelmed with gratitude.

"Ivan, thank you for everything you have done for me, for Mike. You have helped me through some tough times in my life, and I sincerely appreciate it." She gave him a big hug, noticing a slight tear rolling down his cheek.

"Any day, Tahlia, you and Mike have beautiful souls." Ivan melted into the gratitude that Tahlia was extending his way.

Walking down the village, winding her way to the bakery, Tahlia became consumed in thought. *It's strange I've never noticed the little angel before. Maybe it had been in Ivan's bedroom, and he recently moved it to the mantelpiece. Although it does seem an odd coincidence that both Ivan's angel and my mystery angel look very similar.* Tahlia shrugged it off as an image filled her mind. A vision of Ivan's grandmother, sitting by candlelight, lovingly carving the angel, singing in prayer. Tahlia felt her heart expand, an inner beauty pouring out. Gazing around Tahlia sensed this beauty in all things, feeling comforted by an inner knowing life is truly magical.

∞ 26 ∞

JOYFUL ADVENTURES

MIKE AND TAHLIA fell in love with Joyful Adventures; she was a beautiful catamaran and made the perfect home. All the love and care Ivan had put into the boat showed. She was in mint condition with little quirks and squeaks that made her unique, inviting, and a pleasure to sail.

Mike had waited for the best day to sail Tahlia over to Calanques de Cassis. Joyful Adventures looked so grand, her big white sails in full bloom, gliding across the Mediterranean Sea. Tahlia loved the wind billowing in the sails, pushing them along, the crystal-clear water, the smell of the salt air as the sun kissed her skin. She fell in love with Calanques inlets, surrounded by steep rocky cliffs, jutting into the turquoise blue ocean. They were so picturesque. Looking back at the big limestone rock faces, Tahlia felt all her senses becoming heightened, tingling in aliveness. Joyful Adventures was now their new home, one that would take them on many adventures. A big grin beamed across Tahlia's face.

Tahlia headed below deck to grab her hat out of the suitcase. Opening the bag, she found the Joyful Adventures ornament. Tahlia was still intrigued; how could it be that Mike was inspired to create the ornament from the twins' toys, and now they were sailing on a boat named Joyful Adventures? She glanced at the ornament with a twinge in her heart, recalling Jayden and Sierra happily playing with their toys. That life seemed way off in the past. Expelling a big sigh, Tahlia was thankful for the twins' giggling faces regularly appearing, giving her the fuel to live each day to the fullest.

Lost in a moment of reflection, Tahlia remembered what Ivan had said in one of those transport moments. "Life is a gift; it is up to us to unwrap it and live it fully."

Tahlia felt at last that she and Mike were making progress, embarking on a new adventure together. Tahlia couldn't help but wonder, what wonderful magical things will they co-create? She was excited about their future.

"Tahlia, come quick," Mike summoned her with a sense of urgency in his voice.

Tahlia raced up, still hanging onto the twins' ornament. In front of the bow were two dolphins frocking in the waves, playing alongside the boat. Tahlia looked at Mike, a memory of them all swimming with the dolphins in Hawaii came flooding to her mind.

"The twins," they said in unison.

Tahlia hugged the Joyous Adventures ornament to her chest, as the dolphins frolicked and entertained them. Mike and Tahlia, both took it as a sign, sharing an unspoken knowing in their hearts. A certainty that the twins' energy would always be with them, wherever they went, reminding them to find the joy.

***

Tahlia and Mike found the perfect safe place for the Joyful Adventures ornament inside the main cabin. Mike had crafted a padded box to put it in, for whenever they might come across bad weather.

Tahlia and Mike had grown fond of Cassis, yet they knew there were many more discoveries and adventures to experience. It had come time to leave the cute French village they had temporarily made home. Tahlia was a little sad; she had loved getting acquainted with the town and all its nuances. The familiar characters walking up and down the cobblestone streets, women with their scarves, men wearing French berets, walking their dogs, enjoying coffee basking in the morning sun. The wafting scent of fresh baguettes and croissants, children's laughter as they ran up and down in the village.

Tahlia recognized how this routine of familiar faces and lifestyle had helped her feel comfortable stepping into her new life, yet at the same time realized nothing is forever. There would be a lot of endings and new beginnings on this journey.

In Seraphina's words, "Change is the only guarantee in life, and there is always peace and beauty in change."

Waving good-bye to Ivan and Serge, Tahlia knew she would be seeing them again and felt a gentle nudge of reassurance.

Mike navigated Joyous Adventures out of the harbor into their new life. The waters were calm, a gentle breeze carrying the boat forward. Mike and Tahlia relaxed into the smooth sailing with a glass of champagne, celebrating. Tahlia gazed at her wooden angel sitting on the table near them. To this day, she had no real explanation of how her angel mysteriously turned up, yet Tahlia was sure it had a lot to do with the unfolding of her life.

Who would have thought that a failed suicide attempt, alluring blue eyes, strange visions, a mysterious angel, and random synchronicities would have led her to Mike, to this life they had lived? The birth of their twins, so happy and joyous. The painful passing of Jayden and Sierra, which had left a massive void in their hearts, appearing impossible to fill. An endlessly deep canyon, now filled with memories of all the fun times they had spent together as a family.

Thank goodness for all the unexplained magical appearances of Ivan, Serge, and Seraphina, accompanied by such comforting insights.

Tahlia recalled when Seraphina had shown her the moving scale of emotional vibrations, it all made sense now. She saw clearly how Mike and she had moved through that scale. Grief, anger, frustration, sadness, all playing their tunes. These emotions bubbling up, having to be felt and accepted. They had both grown through the pain of feeling trapped and lifeless with no will to live, to a happy place beyond their imaginings. They had discovered from deep within, immeasurable amounts of love, strength, and a renewed enthusiasm for life.

Tahlia looked up from her angel to Mike, his alluring blue eyes, and the smile on his face gave her an inner knowing; this was exactly where they were meant to be.

Tahlia smiled at Mike, raising her glass, "Are you as excited as I am to see what wonderful new adventures we shall co-create?"

Mike nodded, giving her an affectionate kiss.

As she snuggled into the comfort of his body, Tahlia thought, *Life certainly is worth embracing! Even in your darkest hours, there is always a way to surrender to joy.*

∞ SNEAK PEEK ~ NEXT BOOK ∞

SERAPHINA CLICKED HER fingers, and the most beautiful white horse appeared in front of them both.

"Jump on," coaxed Seraphina.

Tahlia mounted the horse bareback as Seraphina hopped on behind her.

Seraphina encouraged the horse forward, "Come on, Freedom, time for an adventure."

Tahlia noted the name of the horse, *Freedom, how appropriate*, she thought.

The beautiful white horse broke into a gallop, her long white mane flowing gracefully. Tahlia felt so incredibly free, galloping along the riverbank, smiling from ear to ear. Seraphina leaned against Tahlia, gently humming, the same melody which always soothed Tahlia's thoughts and heart.

As they raced through the canopy of green trees, both Tahlia and Seraphina's hair flowed in the wind, matching the flow of Freedom's long white mane. Freedoms' strides were long, purposeful, and full of power. The faster they rode, swirling energy whipped up around them. It wasn't a frenzy of energy but more like an energy of passion and excitement, twirling around as if it were sucking the three of them into a magical vortex.

Freedom was spurred on by the swirling energy, cantering through an archway of overhanging rocks, leading onto a pristine golden beach. Aqua-colored water gently lapped the edge of the shoreline, as a silvery light from the rising full moon glistened through the waves. The beach was short, with a cave at the far end. Freedom galloped toward the cave, a faint smell of salt lingering in the air as Freedom's' hooves pounded across the sand, waves chasing her strides.

Slowing, the horse stopped in front of the cave, gracefully bending down, allowing Tahlia and Seraphina to step off her.

"Thank you, Freedom, we won't be long," said Seraphina as she patted the horse affectionately.

"Come on, Tahlia, I want to show you some magic."

Tahlia was excited; she loved the magic of life and any chance to discover something magical always intrigued and drew her in.

Seraphina and Tahlia made their way on foot into the cave, Tahlia could hear the sound of soft dripping water coming from somewhere ahead. In every step Tahlia took, her feet would stumble over rocks, landing on what felt like cold, wet sand.

It took a minute or two for Tahlia's eyes to adjust, making out tiny flickering lights, which appeared to be hovering, illuminating a sandy path between rocky boulders, inside a tunnel. The farther Seraphina and Tahlia made their way into the cave, the louder the dripping water got.

As she got closer to the glowing lights, Tahlia noticed...

End of Prelude

∞ About the Author – Maree Stuartt ∞

As a young child, Maree always had an inner nudging to write. However, not until now with her inner self-acceptance and the accumulation of life experiences has Maree given herself permission to follow her innermost burning passion and write her first novel. It's wonderful now we get to join Maree on her new exciting journey—to write and inspire the hearts of many.

Maree's life has taken her on copious worldwide adventures from solo backpacking, a career in the film industry, successful business's and connecting to others as a dedicated yoga practitioner.

Being a celebrity makeup artist, Maree has spent her entire makeup career looking into people's souls. Along this colourful journey, working with countless people from all walks of life, she realized everyone has a story. Holding a safe space and being a good listener, Maree recognized everyone is searching for Joy.

Each new life experience ignited Maree's fascination with the art of storytelling and equipped her with the ability to paint a picture, evoking the senses, transporting you out of your everyday existence into a sense of awe and delight.

Maree's curious nature is continuously expanding her creativity and imagination, allowing the words to flow, capturing inspiring and captivating moments for the reader. The film industry enhanced Maree's love of storytelling, giving her the clarity on how powerfully a story can transform, inspire and uplift. In many ways, both life and all her worldly experiences have prepared Maree for this next new chapter in her life of writing to empower others.

The loving intention that inspires Maree's writing is to encourage others to live empowering lives through co-creating a life you truly love.

Connect with maree

If you would like to discover ways to work with me, stay connected, or even reach out and say hi, informing me how this book has touched you.

Please head over to www.mareestuartt.com

Until we meet again, I wish you love and happiness.
Cheers maree

www.ingramcontent.com/pod-product-compliance
Lightning Source LLC
Chambersburg PA
CBHW050337110726
47899CB00007B/2542